Praise for the Violet Series

"A story for any girl who ever ... to have her wildest dream come tru...

—*New Yor...* ...ssen

"A fun, fashion-filled, fast-paced read! Violet is a hero for all of us wallflowers." —Carolyn Mackler, bestselling author of *Guyaholic*

"Violet is wonderfully witty and sweetly sensitive. She's not your typical top model; she's more like your best friend—only prettier."
—Kristen Kemp, author of *Breakfast at Bloomingdale's*

"For every girl who's ever looked at a glossy magazine and wanted to know the story behind the picture. Melissa Walker creates fiction couture—unique and beautiful. On the runway or off, Violet shines."
—Ally Carter, bestselling author of *I'd Tell You I Love You,*
But Then I'd Have to Kill You

Praise for Violet on the Runway

"You know it rocks." —ELLEgirl.com

"I couldn't put it down! You're kind of rooting for her to make it big, and kind of rooting for her to just go home before the biz ruins her."
—Glamour.com

"Teens will love this fun fashion read." —*OK! Weekly*

"This novel, about the ins and outs of the fashion business, is a perfect read for teens who want to see what lies beneath the glossy veneer of what seems to be a picture-perfect life." —*Family Circle*

Berkley JAM titles by Melissa Walker

VIOLET ON THE RUNWAY

VIOLET BY DESIGN

violet
BY design

melissa walker

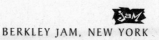
BERKLEY JAM, NEW YORK

THE BERKLEY PUBLISHING GROUP
Published by the Penguin Group
Penguin Group (USA) Inc.
375 Hudson Street, New York, New York 10014, USA
Penguin Group (Canada), 90 Eglinton Avenue East, Suite 700, Toronto, Ontario M4P 2Y3, Canada
(a division of Pearson Penguin Canada Inc.)
Penguin Books Ltd., 80 Strand, London WC2R 0RL, England
Penguin Group Ireland, 25 St. Stephen's Green, Dublin 2, Ireland (a division of Penguin Books Ltd.)
Penguin Group (Australia), 250 Camberwell Road, Camberwell, Victoria 3124, Australia
(a division of Pearson Australia Group Pty. Ltd.)
Penguin Books India Pvt. Ltd., 11 Community Centre, Panchsheel Park, New Delhi—110 017, India
Penguin Group (NZ), 67 Apollo Drive, Rosedale, North Shore 0632, New Zealand
(a division of Pearson New Zealand Ltd.)
Penguin Books (South Africa) (Pty.) Ltd., 24 Sturdee Avenue, Rosebank, Johannesburg 2196,
South Africa

Penguin Books Ltd., Registered Offices: 80 Strand, London WC2R 0RL, England

VIOLET BY DESIGN

This book is an original publication of The Berkley Publishing Group.

This is a work of fiction. Names, characters, places, and incidents either are the product of the author's imagination or are used fictitiously, and any resemblance to actual persons, living or dead, business establishments, events, or locales is entirely coincidental. The publisher does not have any control over and does not assume any responsibility for author or third-party websites or their content.

PRINTING HISTORY
Berkley JAM trade paperback edition / March 2008

Berkley trade paperback ISBN: 978-0-425-21940-9

An application to register this book for cataloging has been submitted to the Library of Congress.

PRINTED IN THE UNITED STATES OF AMERICA

10 9 8 7 6 5 4 3 2 1

For Johnny, Tim, and Kristi,
who made it fun to be the baby sister.

acknowledgments

My family and friends deserve big hugs for making me feel like a rockstar author at all times. I'm grateful to Kate Seaver, my editor, and Doug Stewart, my agent, for their ever wise book-world advice. And huge thanks to Kristin Mahoney, who is always up for reading and responding to my work, even in its very roughest form.

one

"What do you think, Violet—dark purple?" Julie asks.

"Uh, sure," I say, not turning to look at my best friend's DIY pedicure setup. I'm leaning back in a plastic lounge chair at my neighborhood pool, trying to relax during my last week at home in Chapel Hill, North Carolina. Unfortunately, I'm not that good at relaxing because I'm also trying to look cool in my new, psychedelic-colored Dona Pink designer bikini. In one week I'll be walking down a runway in Brazil to model his bathing suits, so why do I feel like I can't even pull this one off at my local swim club?

Even with my Chanel sunglasses and my jeweled flip-flops and this $1,000 bikini, I have to admit that I still feel like the gawky girl by the side of the pool. The one who never even took her T-shirt off to swim before this summer, the one who knew being six feet one and a size 2 was a crazy liability in the high school world where fitting in is all that matters, the one who once longed to be part of the popular clique—the BK, short for the Bee's Knees. But all that seems so long ago. And even though it's only been like ten months since I was that girl, so much has changed.

When I signed with Tryst Models last year, I hoped it would make me popular at Chapel Hill High School—and I guess it kinda did—but I was missing the big picture. You know, the one where I'd move to New York, live in a model apartment, make out with a club promoter, have a drug-addicted bulimic roommate, and then quit modeling altogether—only to be enticed back into the madness by the promise of a trip to Brazil for São Paulo Fashion Week (that would be the fashion show I'm supposed to be doing in, oh, seven days). I have a weakness for international travel, especially since I've never been off the East Coast. Wow—when I run through the last year in my head like that, it seems more like a clichéd TV movie than my actual life.

"*Vioooleet!* Focus!" snaps Julie, who probably knows that I'm still thinking about how nervous the prospect of the Brazilian runway is making me. "This is important. So. Purple or black polish for my toes?"

"Why don't you just wear . . . *Brown*," says a voice behind us. Julie turns to roll her eyes at the third member of our best-friend trio, Roger. Brown University is exactly where Julie will be starting college in a month.

"Funny, Roger," says Julie. "Seriously, Violet, I need your opinion. Soon I won't have my international runway star around to advise me on fashion choices—and I want to make the best impression possible during freshman orientation."

I smile. Knowing Julie's type-A personality, she's probably already plotted her first week of outfits for the Brown campus, complete with trendy belts and boots and tights that will look great on her petite frame, plus dresses and sweaters in intense fall blues, which will be stunning next to her long, dark hair and her eternally tan skin. I, on the other hand, am leaving in less than a week but haven't packed a thing. It's winter in Brazil, and I have no idea what to wear.

"I'll tell you what *not* to wear to orientation," Roger chimes in, pulling up a lounge chair next to mine.

"Do tell, fashion boy," says Julie.

"Giant logo sunglasses," says Roger, nodding his head in my direction.

"Oh shut up!" I laugh. "These were free! And I thought they would be fun to wear, like, in Brazil."

"Or, say, at the Heritage Hills neighborhood pool?" says Roger. "Yes, you fit right in with the Wal-Mart bathing suits. Of course, if there's someone here you're trying to impress . . ."

I see Roger look over to the other side of the patio, where the BK girls—Shelly Ryan, Jasmine Jostling, and Tina Geiger—are ordering french fries from the concession stand. I roll my eyes to convey that I'm so done with working to impress them. "Please, Roger," I say. "High school is over."

"So true," says Julie, putting on a mock serious face. "We're college students now. Well, two college students and one will-be Vassar girl, at least."

I smile and fish my digital camera out of my bag, pulling Roger and Julie in for a self-taken close-up.

"Adorable," pronounces Julie as she grabs the camera to check out the photo. "Now, can we get back to my toes here?"

"How about sparkling navy?" I say, pulling a L'Oréal sample out of my bag. "Veronica just sent me some swag from her last beauty shoot—this color is going to be huge in the fall."

"See, that's what I'm talking about," says Julie, grabbing the bottle from my hands.

"So how *is* Veronica?" asks Roger. Veronica was one of my roommates last year in the model apartment—the one with the, um, nose candy problem as well as a nasty eating disorder. But she's also a pretty famous model—and, after a lot of hard work and a few knife-in-the-back moments, I consider her a friend.

"She's good," I say, and I think it's the truth. Veronica got out of rehab in June and she has her own apartment in Brooklyn now. "I think she might even be coming to Brazil, but I'm not sure yet."

"So is this one of the bikinis you'll be showing off down there?" asks Roger, glancing at my orange-and-yellow-swirled bathing suit.

"Uh, no," I say, feeling my face flush. "This one's from last year. They just sent me a few samples." I can't help the blushing, and I have to fight the urge to pull on my oversized T-shirt. Things have been weird with Roger lately. Not bad weird, exactly, but just . . . different. He and Julie have been my best friends since we were five years old and got placed together for "centers"—where you move around from cooking station to math station to art station in kinder-garten. And they still are my best friends, but something has changed between me and Roger since he surprised me in New York last year with a visit and then took me to the prom, which was a lot more fun than I expected.

I'm probably just being overdramatic. I mean, this summer has been weird in general, which makes sense since it's the last summer before we all split up—Roger's heading to the city to attend NYU and Julie will be in Providence, Rhode Island. I've got this Brazil trip—I deferred my admission to Vassar until the spring semester so I can try to book some of the fall fashion shows in Europe. My agent, Angela Blythe, told me that after I make my São Paulo debut I might even be able to book something in Milan or Paris. Honestly, I'm more excited about seeing the world than stomping down run-ways, but if that's what gets me the plane ticket, I'm game.

The fashion scene seems far away when I'm here, though. Thank God. All summer I've been with Julie and Roger—hanging out at the pool, dropping in on my former job at the Palace movie theater (for free movies, of course) and riding around in Julie's old VW Rabbit. I've been working on a guaranteed tearjerker playlist for the past month on iTunes so I can make sure my two best friends both have the perfect musical soundtrack for how much I'm going to miss them.

"So what do you think?" Julie lifts up her freshly painted midnight-blue toenails. "Runway ready?"

"No doubt, Jules," says Roger, putting his hands behind his head and leaning back in his chair. "Now do mine. Just the big toes, I think. That's very fashion forward." A normal eighteen-year-old guy would be joking, but since Julie and I know Roger is totally up for blue toenails ("The better to fit in at NYU," he says), we both grab a foot and start painting. Roger's been a hipster long before any of us even know what that term meant. He was never popular in high school, but he had his own nerdy-chic style going on. He is actually pretty cute, I admit, as I glance up at his face, blue eyes forever framed with thick, dark-rimmed glasses and a mop of fully pomaded black hair. He smiles at me and winks. *He's totally going to rule NYU with that grin*, I think to myself.

When I get back to my house, which is just down the street from the neighborhood pool, Dad is cooking dinner. "Did you have a good swim, Violet?" he asks, turning away from the puttanesca sauce he has simmering on the stove. "Yes, Dad," I say, giving him a kiss on the cheek before I head upstairs to my room. I kind of love how he still talks to me in the same voice he's used since I was eight years old.

I glance in the full-length mirror on the back of my door as it closes. It's true that I've always been freak-tall and über-thin—to the point where people made fun of me almost all through junior high and high school, until this whole modeling thing came along. But I still find it hard to believe that the Violet Greenfield I see in *Teen Girl* magazine fashion spreads (April issue, thank you very much) is the same Violet Greenfield in the mirror of my childhood bedroom. Sure, I shed the wire-frame glasses for contacts or way-cooler reddish-black frames, but I still see the same dishwater-blond hair (now stringy from that overchlorinated pool), big

Mickey Mouse ears, and knobby knees that I've resented since sixth grade.

I lean in to examine my pasty, freckled face. Last year I learned how to do a smoky eye really well so that my pale green eyes seem more brilliant jade than faded gray (which is how I always saw them growing up). I look down at the note Julie taped on my mirror—a tactic her life coach is fond of. It reads, "THE WORLD SEES A SUPER-MODEL." It's supposed to remind me to let go of the insecurities that plague me and embrace my destiny as a queen of fashion. That's how Julie put it anyway.

I grab a towel and my bathrobe and head down the hall to the shower. Before I leave my room though, I take one more glance in the mirror. I even flash myself a smile. I don't see a supermodel, but I've come a long way from last year when I saw a capital-L Loser.

"Violet, honey, Angela called today," says Mom as I sit down at the dinner table. I sigh. I'm glad Mom is handling my agent's requests, which come fast and furious—especially as the Brazil dates approach. Last week Angela asked if I couldn't just pop up to New York City to get my highlights done, her treat. Julie was jumping up and down and asking if she could tag along, but all I wanted to do was scream, "No!"

I haven't been back to the city since I left the model apartment in May—that was after Veronica's drug overdose and my breakup with Peter Heller, nightclub promoter/NYU student/Class A dickweed. I found out that Peter wasn't even really a student at NYU—he just took some continuing ed classes. His family's super rich, though, so that got him in with every club in the city. So lame. I just don't want to go back there—at least not for a while.

I told Mom to tell Angela that Brazil was where I'd see her—I'm only getting back on this crazy modeling merry-go-round for the travel perks. You know how you read interviews with models in magazines (which are inevitably super boring) and they always say what they like most about modeling is "the travel"? Well, there you go. I guess I'm a stereotypical model.

"Does Angela want me to just hop up to Soho for a manicure tomorrow?" I ask sarcastically as I dig into Dad's pasta. "Mmm, good!" interrupts my brother Jake through a spaghetti-filled mouth. I have a feeling he's sick of Tryst Models talk at the dinner table. Until recently, he was the star of mealtime conversations since he plays on the varsity basketball team in high school. This year he'll be a junior, and I'm sure he's glad I'll be out of the house so he can reclaim our parents' full attention. Jake and Julie were dating this summer, but she's trying to distance herself since she's leaving for college now, so I have a lot of sympathy for my brother these days.

My mom, however—though loving and kind—has never tapped into the nuances of her children's emotions. "No," she says, addressing my question and ignoring Jake's food critique. "Angela says a crew from *Teen Fashionista* wants to follow you around for a day. You know, in your home environment."

"And I guess you told her there's no time for that?" I say, eyes widening. "I mean, I'm leaving here in like five days and I have a million things to do. When could they possibly come?"

Mom smiles sheepishly. "Honey, Angela was really insistent that this one was important," she says, looking at Dad for support as he tucks into his pasta and avoids eye contact. "You've been putting her off all summer, and she *is* giving you this big trip to Brazil and all."

My parents don't understand that my agent doesn't "give" me anything. It's all about making money and raising the profile for Tryst—it's not like she's some generous cousin who's lavishing me with gifts. But I know this argument is lost on them.

"So . . . what are you telling me?" I ask, afraid to hear the answer.

"A reporter and photographer will be here in the morning," says Mom. "At eight A.M."

two

My alarm goes off at seven fifteen A.M., which is completely crazy for a summer morning. I washed my hair last night and I know it's not good to overshampoo, so I jump in the shower for a wake-up rinse-off. Back in my room holding a towel to my chest, I stare blankly at my closet, unable to form thoughts about what to wear. *Teen Fashionista* is the most stylish of the teen magazines—it's actually pretty flattering that they want to spend a day with me, and I have to admit that I got a little excited last night as I IMed with Julie about what we could do today to seem cool. We decided that we'd stop at the Palace for a free movie (and free popcorn, if we bring our own bowl), then go eat at Allen and Son's, this great, rustic restaurant on the edge of town that serves amazing barbecue and hush puppies—not to mention sweet tea. Finally, we'll end up over at Roger's, because he's got the nicest house. His parents are loaded.

Ding-dong.

Julie's at the door wearing a cute Marc Jacobs dress that I *know* she bought on eBay. I don't have the heart to tell her that I bet the *Teen Fashionista* people will notice it's from two years ago. But she looks really pretty and I'm annoyed with myself for even *knowing* it's from two years ago, so I stay quiet.

"Cute!" I say as she rushes in, a complete ball of energy even at this ungodly hour.

"Violet, you're not ready!" she gasps, grabbing my hand and pulling me up the stairs to my room.

"We have half an hour," I say, realizing as I take a closer look at Julie that not only has she straightened her naturally wavy hair, but then she curled it to make extra-smooth waves. And her makeup must have taken an hour. "Good Lord, Jules," I say. "You look like you're styled for a cover shoot."

"Hello!" she shouts, way too loudly for this time of day. "It's *Teen Fashionista!* Get excited. Besides, they may want some friend shots, right?"

I guess my nonchalance must be kind of exasperating, since Julie is completely ecstatic about the day. *Have I really become jaded?* I wonder. I pull on a black-and-white striped cotton minidress. Julie shakes her head. "Not special, Violet," she says. "Semi *Factory Girl,* but kind of boring."

"I'm not done yet," I say, reaching into the back of my closet for my magic-feather Prada boots. Black-and-brown leather, knee-high, with a platform heel. I got these as a present from Angela last year on my first trip to New York, and I swear they helped me book runway shows. I walk taller in them—and not just because the heel is crazy high.

Ding-dong.

They're early? Magazine people are never early. Julie and I freeze and listen to my dad pad down the stairs—probably in his robe and slippers, I realize in horror. But before I can race to the door, I hear him talking to a woman with an incredibly bubbly voice. She sounds more like a BK girl than a magazine editor.

When I peek around the stairwell, I see a short, blond, curly-headed girl with a notebook, along with a sandy-haired photographer who looks about Michael J. Fox's height.

"Violet?!" squeals the curly girl, who looks about my age. "I'm so happy to meet you!" She holds out her hand and shakes mine vigorously. "I'm an assistant editor at *Teen Fashionista*, and this is my first profile. I am super excited." Then she starts walking slowly around my living room, scribbling notes, presumably about our lackluster beige carpet and the awful, plaid overstuffed chair that my dad won't let my mom re-cover.

I look over at Julie, who shrugs. I don't know what I was expecting in a *Teen Fashionista* reporter, but this girl was not it. On the upside, she seems less intimidating than I thought she'd be. But now the photographer guy is asking to take a picture of me and Dad, who, of course, *is* in his blue robe and brown slippers.

"Sure!" says my father, holding up his #1 DAD coffee mug and slinging his other arm around me. "Smile, Violet!" I hope my face isn't conveying what I'm thinking: *I will die if this ends up in the magazine.*

I don't have time to do anything with my hair, so I pull it into a loose ponytail and slip on a black headband. Then it's the quick makeup trick my roommate Sam taught me last year—blue mascara and a touch of red lip stain—and we're out the door. I'm expecting a limo or at least a Town Car like Tryst's driver Mario used to pick me up in when I lived in New York, but all I see is a rented Ford Focus parked behind Julie's Rabbit.

"Let's take your car!" yells the assistant editor, whose name I now know is Chloe. "It'll be authentic."

"Well, it's Julie's car," I say.

"Whatever," she says, motioning for the photographer to take a shot of me with the Rabbit. I pull Julie into the frame and we put on our best smiles. This is going to be a long day.

At the Palace, where I spent two years of my life donning a vest and bow tie to serve popcorn and tear tickets, my old manager Richard greets us at the door. He's wearing a navy suit and large Christian Dior sunglasses, which is ridiculous because he's normally in a T-shirt and khakis. I called him last night to make sure it was cool for me and Julie and the *Teen Fashionista* crew to come in and see a movie. I guess he thought this was his big break, so he's decked out in flamboyant glory.

"Violet, little flower, how *are* you?" he asks, in a totally exaggerated Southern drawl.

"Fine, Richard," I say, smiling at Joanie, the overweight woman in the ticket booth who is waving excitedly.

"Are we in a movie?!" I hear her shouting from inside the booth.

"No, Joanie!" screams Julie. "It's just a regular camera."

I guess I forgot that the theater crowd might be a little embarrassing. I can see Chloe writing furiously on her flip-top notepad, which makes me nervous, so I link my arm through hers and bring her inside to stop the pen movement.

"So you used to work here?" Chloe asks, taking in the spotted black carpet and the giant candy counters.

"Uh, yeah," I say. "Like after school and during the summer."

"Cool!" she chirps. I can't get a read on whether she's really peppy or really sarcastic.

"Violet, man, what's up?" I hear a slow, deep voice behind me and I know it's Benny, a stoner college student who I used to work with here. He was actually a pretty good advice-giver on six-hour shifts, which involve about fifteen minutes of work every two hours at showtime.

"Benny!" I lean in to give him a hug and Michael J. Fox snaps a photo. The photographer's name is actually Michael, I found out, which amuses me. But I'm annoyed that he's taking pictures in here. I guess I wanted the *Teen Fashionista* people to incorporate the "Violet sees free movies" angle in the story—not "Violet had a dorky first job." And no way I'm revealing that I still sub a rare shift for kicks, even though I have a few thousand dollars saved from last spring's modeling. I just kind of love the atmosphere and the quirky people at the Palace. But I'd never admit that to *Teen Fashionista*.

"Oh, Violet, let's get one of me and you!" says Richard. "You know, I'm her runway mentor," he whispers loudly to Chloe as he grabs my arm to pull me in for a photo. "That's R-I-C-H-A . . ."

"Ooh, me too!" says Joanie, bounding out of the box to lean into a picture that I am absolutely positive will never grace the pages of *Teen Fashionista*. "Smile pretty!" says Richard.

The theater was a good idea in the end—despite the cast of characters Chloe met—because watching a movie sucked up two hours of time where she and Michael didn't get to catalog every word or movement I made.

Now we're driving to Allen and Son's for lunch. As we pull into the gravel driveway, Chloe exclaims, "Oh, how country!" I fight the urge to grimace.

Julie and I had a moment to exchange opinions in the movie theater bathroom, and we came to the conclusion that Chloe's completely annoying. She also snorts when she laughs—a big honking snort like you might see on an exaggeration-prone comedy show. Still, I don't want her to dislike me at all—then she might write a bad profile—so I'm using my New York modeling world tricks and being fake-nice to her. Julie's been a school leader for so long that her diplomacy skills are tack-sharp. Chloe *loves* us.

We talk over lunch about what a typical Chapel Hill day is like, which is such a ridiculous premise. I mean, it's just like . . . life.

There's not a succinct outline for it. But Julie and I manage to concoct some silly schedule like, "Oh, we see movies, come eat barbecue, stroll around the University of North Carolina campus . . ." as if that's what we do day after day after day. Chloe eats it up.

Michael shoots five rolls of film in Allen and Son's—I knew they'd love the taxidermy on the walls, not to mention the plastic red-and-white checkered tablecloths—and then we pile in the Rabbit again to go see Roger. I'm kind of disappointed when Chloe doesn't want to stay at his huge house and shoot some photos there—I guess I thought she'd want that wealthy angle, though it's not me who's rich. Instead, we pick up Roger and head for the Carolina campus for what Michael calls "group friend shots."

"People from Chapel Hill call the university 'Carolina,'" I explain to Chloe, who's now used up two full notepads on the details of our fairly boring afternoon. We find a parking spot pretty easily on Franklin Street, and Roger goes on and on about how lovely it is when the students are away for the summer and how parking is Chapel Hill's biggest issue, blah, blah, blah. Chloe is giggling and taking down every word, though I can't imagine why that inane information would be useful to *Teen Fashionista* readers.

When we get out of the car, we all start walking toward the Old Well, which is this small dome supported by white columns in the middle of campus. It's like the symbol of Carolina and there are grass-and-brick paths around it, so it's pretty collegiate-looking. As we pose for "natural" shots where the three of us are walking together, then sitting together and talking, then fake laughing on the steps of the Old Well, Roger whispers, "It's like we're shooting publicity stills for *One Tree Hill*!" Then Julie and I crack up for real.

"More like a college catalog shoot," I say.

"Nah, we have no diversity here," says Julie. "I have never seen a college catalog photo with all white people."

"What are you guys talking about?" asks Chloe, leaning closer to catch our conversation without blocking the shot.

"Nothing!" we chime together. This actually feels like a pretty fun day. I make a mental note to ask Chloe for some outtakes from the shoot.

Julie drops off Roger first, which makes the backseat considerably more comfortable for Chloe and Michael, who looks like he's about to be sick. He's been totally quiet all day, and I wonder if he dislikes Chloe as much as Julie and I do. Surprisingly, Roger didn't make one caustic remark about Chloe—but maybe he was just afraid of her being in earshot, which she pretty much was all day.

When we get to my house, I wave good-bye to Julie and invite Chloe and Michael inside. I'm relieved when they decline.

"We should get back to the hotel—we're flying out really early tomorrow morning," says Chloe. "But it was *sooooo* great to spend the day with you and your friends."

"Thanks," I say, glad my last moments of being graciously "on" are upon me. "It was really nice to meet you guys."

I'm shaking her hand good-bye when Chloe floors me. "Hey, do you mind if I get Roger's number?" she giggles. "You know, for follow-up."

"Uh, sure," I say, feeling annoyed. I recite the number as she programs it into her cell, which seems unnecessary. Now it's, like, there forever and her phone list will read "Roger" as if he's some friend of hers or something.

Ew.

The next few days go by in a blur. I'm trying to work in time with Roger and Julie, of course, but also with my family—Mom has been a little manic about me going to Brazil and we *just* got my passport and visa yesterday. I've never been out of the country before, and I think I'm almost as nervous as my mother, who's sitting on my bed as I finish packing.

"Your warm coat should be a carry-on, Violet," she says, as I try to stuff a puffy jacket into my already overflowing suitcase. It's so weird that it's like a hundred degrees here but it's winter in Brazil. Roger scoffed at me when I questioned that, saying, "It's below the equator, dummy," as if that's supposed to explain *everything*. I want to say to Mom that I don't really feel like carrying a heavy coat around the Raleigh-Durham airport, but I'm also so tired of squabbling with her about the details of this trip that I give in and take it out of the suitcase. It probably wasn't going to fit anyway.

"Okay," I say, tossing the jacket aside and popping down on top of the suitcase to help pull the zipper closed.

Mom leans down to the floor and helps me finish the final zip. "Done!" I exclaim. When I look over at her there are tears in her eyes. "Uh-oh," I say. "What?"

"Nothing." Mom sniffles. "It's just that my little girl is going out into the real world. I'm proud of you, Violet."

"Aw, Mom," I say, reaching out to give her a sitting-on-the-floor hug. "I was in New York last year—so it's like the same thing."

"No, Violet," she says. "This is a brand-new adventure."

three

My flight to São Paulo is, like, fourteen hours long with a stopover in Miami, and I find myself tearing up as I listen to the playlist I made for Julie and Roger. I know it's extremely nerdy to get emotional over *your own playlist*, but I swear when Pink Floyd's "Wish You Were Here" comes on I think I'm going to have to shut myself in the tiny plane bathroom and use up all the tissues.

Saying good-bye to Julie was tough. She actually made me go back to high school—the place we'd left just two months ago—to take pictures on campus. I made her snap one in front of my locker, which is super dorky, but I wanted to remember one special detail. During sophomore year, someone wrote "I ❤ VIOLET GREENFIELD" in small black letters right on the silver metal above my lock. I never found out who did it, but that scrawl and the idea of a secret admirer got me through some major low-confidence days, so I needed a photo.

After our nostalgia-for-the-very-near-past session, I spent the night at Julie's house like I've been doing since about first grade, and of course we had to flip through the yearbook and make snide comments about what people might be doing in ten years (the BK girls, we decided, should put their moniker—and their three collective brain cells—to use and work the Burger King drive-up window). We talked until about four A.M., when we both fell asleep on the foldout bed. In the morning I left really early because I couldn't stand the thoughts running through my head about this being the last time I'd sleep over like this, before college and the real world and all that growing-up stuff comes along.

After leaving Julie's, I drove over to Roger's to deliver the mix CD, which I called "Last Goodbye" after our favorite Jeff Buckley song (and because I'm completely over the top like that). I handed it to him and he said, "I will cycle each and every one of these songs through my MySpace profile, in tribute to you." Then he pulled me into his chest and we just stood in his driveway hugging. I could feel his sweater getting wet as I teared up, and I stepped back and sniffled, saying something about how I didn't want to ruin an Original Penguin. He looked at me for a second and then pulled me back in without saying a word. We hugged for a good ten minutes in total silence before I finally got in the car drove away.

It sounds weird, but I'm not just going on vacation or away for summer camp—we're all *leaving* now. And although I don't doubt that we'll be friends forever, I know it'll never be the same as it was when we were growing up at home. And I feel like that time ended, like, today.

And now that I'm on the plane listening to the Killers sing "When You Were Young," I'm in complete mourn mode for my best friends. So finally I just put away my iPod and try to sleep.

By the time I go through baggage claim and customs in São Paulo, I'm so tired that I can barely read my own name, which is on a sign being held by a short, gray-haired man with a curled-up mustache. We pantomime a bit to determine that, yes, I am Violet Greenfield. Lamely, I was thinking my high school Spanish might be useful in Brazil, but—duh—they speak Portuguese here.

As we drive through the city, I can't help but think it looks a lot like New York—giant buildings everywhere, crowds and busy streets, bicycles weaving in and out of traffic. When we pull up to the Hotel Mirna, I feel like a little girl pretending she's old enough to be jet-setting and staying in fancy places. The concierge speaks English perfectly, and as the bellhop rides up to my room with me, I get a tingle of excitement. I am in *another country*. I look down at my brown suede ballet flats and flash back to them walking down my driveway just this morning. Now they're standing in an old-fashioned, gold-gilt-covered elevator in *Brazil*.

We get off the elevator on the seventh floor, and I realize the whole hotel opens in the middle around a giant, curving staircase like in *Gone With the Wind*—which, okay, is my secret favorite movie. (My public favorite movie is *The Royal Tenenbaums*, which, while a great film with infinitely more cool cred, is no *Gone With the Wind*). The man helping me with my bag—who is wearing a red military jacket that doesn't look that far off from what I wore on a runway last winter—opens the door to room 704 and places my suitcase on a folding wooden luggage stand that looks like it's from my grandmother's house—in a good way. Then he bows and holds out his hand. I shake it, smiling at him and saying, "*obrigada*," which is the one word the cabdriver managed to drill into my head—it means "thank you." Then he shuffles out the door and I turn around and take a deep breath.

My room is gorgeous. Tiny, but "just lovely," as I can hear my mom saying. Burnt-orange organza curtains hang across a huge window that looks out onto the sparkling São Paulo skyline, the shower is all glass, and there are silver beads on the outside of the panel that faces the bed, which I suppose is for the illusion of privacy. The bathroom floors are marble, and I find out after playing

with an assortment of buttons on the wall that they are also—
dramatic pause—*heated!* My feet are always cold, so I especially ap-
preciate the warmth. I have a little refrigerator with candy and water
and wine in it—not to mention a giant fruit bowl on the desk in the
corner, where apples and oranges and grapes and bananas are arranged
around a large bottle of champagne.

But the really exciting stuff is on my bed. Not my bed itself,
which is cute and covered with a grass-patterned green-and-gray
down comforter, but what's *on* my bed. Presents! There must be fifty
bags with tissue paper sticking out of the tops—blue and pink and
yellow and green, all with tags that say "Violet Greenfield" or "Bela
Violeta" or simply "VG," which sort of looks cool in calligraphy. Inside are invitations to attend fashion shows, personal letters from
designers, and lots—I mean lots—of free stuff. A pair of dark-wash
high-waist jeans from Ellys, an amazing long-sleeved eyelet lace
dress from Ingrid Cupola, and four new bikinis from Dona Pink, to
name a few things. As I tear through package after package, I think
I feel a swag headache coming on. This must be how movie stars feel
when they get their Oscar gift bags. I lie back on the tissue paper
with a sigh.

Brring, brring. The phone does a double-time ring and totally
scares me. I haven't called my parents yet to give them my number—
who else could it be? I reach over to grab it. "Hello?"

"Valiant Violet." It's my agent.

"Hi, Angela," I say, almost happy to hear her voice. I was worried
I was going to have to stumble through "You've got the wrong number" in Portuguese.

"Darling, what's that rustling?" she asks.

"Uh, gift bags," I say sheepishly, wondering if it's weird to open
all of them at once like it's Christmas morning. I bet most international runway models are so used to the presents that they just put
them aside and barely glance at the goodies. I'm so not at that too-
cool point, and I kind of doubt I ever will be.

"Well, get yourself out of that mess," Angela orders. "We've got an appointment at the hotel spa in five minutes. I'll see you downstairs."

Click. Ooh, the spa sounds nice. I pull on my yoga pants and a T-shirt and head downstairs.

"Greetings, Sporty Spice," says Angela as she air-kisses both my cheeks. She doesn't say it in a nice way. Her blond hair is perfectly highlighted and blown out, as always, and her gleaming red lipstick matches well-manicured hands. "You know, even at the spa we do like to wear real clothes."

I feel my shoulders start to shrink in a little. I forgot how much Angela's criticisms sting sometimes.

"Oh, toughen up, Vulnerable Violet," she says. "You'll need thick skin for this appointment."

"What is it for?" I ask, suddenly terrified.

"What else?" says Angela, smiling wickedly. "A Brazilian!"

After a few tears and some pitiful whining, I agreed that it did make sense for me to go through with the ritual of torture known as the Brazilian bikini wax, and that Brazil was probably the best place to do it. I am modeling swimsuits, after all. Angela said she knew she'd have to drag me kicking and screaming to the table, so she hadn't dared ask me to get one on my own at home. "Besides," she said, "who knows what those country-bumpkin spa women would have done to you."

Back in my hotel room, I'm lotioning and icing my throbbing, red bikini line. Oh yes, it hurt. When I walked back through the lobby with Angela, I looked like a cowboy in a John Wayne movie who'd been riding his horse for ten days straight. Just as the pain is starting to subside, my phone rings.

"Get dressed," Angela barks. "I'll meet you in the lobby in five."

"Dressed?" I stammer.

"For dinner, of course," snaps Angela. "We'll be dining with a few designers and some other Tryst girls tonight."

I can feel my underarms start to sweat as my heart beats faster.

"Oh, and Violet?" purrs Angela. "When you're putting together your outfit, think Lower East Side—not Lower Atlantic Coast." And then she's gone.

And I'm panicked.

I slip on a simple black shift dress with long sleeves, but I leave my coat in the room. Contrary to my mom's assessment that the July winter in Brazil would be cold, it only dips into the sixties at night—and it's like seventy during the day, I hear. Guess I should have Googled that one myself. Dinner is in the garden of a restaurant just down the block from the hotel, which is good because I'm wearing red patent leather heels that are "too cute for words" according to Julie, but "too painful for words" according to me. Still, I trust my best friend's assessment and I want to look good tonight. I manage to walk normally because the trauma of my wax experience has faded somewhat, and I even put on a long gold chain necklace that Veronica once told me was "edgy but feminine," so I feel like I'm pulling off the look Angela wanted. When she sees me, however, she just chirps, "Well, good enough!" before she hurries me out the door of the hotel. So much for my confidence.

The restaurant is called Spot and we're seated at a long table in front of the blue-green-yellow Brazilian flag, which is as ubiquitous here as the American flag is in rural parts of North Carolina. The room is enclosed in glass, and the crowd of beautiful people is buzzing with energy. I like it, because it reminds me that I'm in a completely new world where I should take everything in.

But what I'm taking in now are all the girls at the table, some of whom are chattering in Portuguese and others who are sitting sullenly, staring at the bread basket with longing eyes. I guess that's what I'm doing too, but only because I don't want to be the only one who eats the bread.

I glance around the table and try to remember a few of the flurry of names Angela rattled off when we sat down. There's Amelia and Lucy, models from New York whom I've seen before but who completely intimidate me with their vacant eyes, and then two Brazilian models with exotic names—Vidonia and Yelena maybe? I can't remember who is who. At the far end of the table is Dona Pink himself, the flamboyant bikini designer who requested me for his show and single-handedly relaunched my modeling career with the promise of this trip to Brazil. He has unkempt black hair that frames his ultratan face a bit wildly, and he's wearing a button-down shirt that is open almost to the navel. He sort of seems like a gay Brazilian Elvis, which is pretty entertaining. He sees me looking at him and raises his glass, shouting, "Violeta!" at which all the other girls reluctantly pick up their drinks and join the toast to me. I blush a little and hold up my Caipirinha, which is a traditional Brazilian drink that tastes limey and has a lot of sugar in it. Translation: I love it. And I've already had two to calm my nerves.

I'm sitting next to Angela at the edge of the table when someone takes the head seat on my left. I look over and see the deepest brown eyes I've seen since my neighbor's golden retriever's. I know it sounds odd to compare person eyes to dog eyes, but believe me, it's a compliment. He also has this adorable, shiny, floppy brown hair that falls just above his shoulders. The guy, not the dog. And he's got big, soft pink lips. "Hello, Violet," he says quietly as he sits down, as though he wants only me to hear his greeting. I feel my eyelashes flutter involuntarily, and I nervously place my hand on my drink to steady its shaking. Suddenly I am acutely aware of how bare I feel, uh, down there. *Am I drunk?* I wonder. Although I did learn to throw a few back in New York last year, I didn't really drink all summer in North Carolina. My tolerance must be way low.

"Hello," I respond, wishing I knew his name too, but so flattered he knows who I am. After going through life as a high school wall-flower, it's still a shock when people get my name right—even now. Especially people who are, oh, drop-dead gorgeous.

Then Beautiful Boy begins to speak: "My name is . . ."

"Paulo!" Dona suddenly notices Beautiful Boy and stands up to greet him. Then all the models' heads turn and my private moment with Beautiful B—Paulo—is over. *Sigh*.

"Dona," Paulo says, smiling and switching into Portuguese so I have absolutely no idea what's going on. Luckily, all-knowing Angela leans in to whisper. "That's Paulo Forte. He's nineteen but he already has his own clothing line because his parents are both big names in Brazilian fashion. He's making a splash, but if you ask me it's only because reporters like the Teen Designer angle—he hasn't shown anywhere but São Paulo yet and you're not big unless you get to . . . Paulo! Mwah! Mwah!"

Angela interrupts her skewering of Paulo to bend over me and air-kiss his cheeks as I lean back to get out of the way of her ever-astounding fakeness.

"You just *must* talk to Violet, Paulo," coos Angela. "You know, she's the next big thing up in New York and she'll be making her international debut in Dona's show tomorrow."

"I have heard," says Paulo, turning his gaze on me once again. I'm melting. "I will enjoy getting to know you, I believe." Okay, now I'm in full swoon mode and I can feel tongue paralysis coming on. I impulsively reach out for a piece of bread to occupy myself, and Paulo says, "I love beautiful girls with an appetite." I smile through chews as I stare down at my third drink, feeling giddy.

As I'm trying to think of something to talk about, I finish off the drink and signal to the waiter for another. I hear the Brazilian girls talking with Dona at the other end of the table. "What are they saying?" I ask Paulo.

"They are talking about the bad—the tragedy—of the model who died of the eating problem," he says.

"I read about that," I say, thinking of my old roommate Veronica and her habit of sticking the back end of a toothbrush down her throat after meals. This Brazilian model had been anorexic, just eating grapes and carrots at the end until her organs failed. I reach for another piece of bread.

"You are healthy," Paulo declares. "Naturally thin."

"I'm lucky, I guess," I say, thinking about how *unlucky* I used to feel in junior high and high school when people made fun of me for being a toothpick-legged giraffe girl. But the modeling world has a different value set.

And then I notice that Amelia and Lucy are staring across the table at me. "So, Lucky Violet," starts Amelia, "still a virgin?"

I can tell she and Lucy are both drunk already—but I'm still not ready for her bold inquiry. I manage a meek "None of your business" as Amelia turns to Paulo.

"You know, sweet little Violet got herself in a few newspapers last year," says Amelia pointedly. I know she's talking about when I went out clubbing with Veronica and was dating that sleaze Peter Heller. The *New York Post* did a gossipy story with quotes from Peter and Veronica about how naïve I was. Veronica even speculated on my virginity, which—hello!—is a sensitive topic, especially since I've only kissed like two guys and I never got past second base with Peter. Is that completely freakish for being eighteen? Do Brazilians read the *New York Post*? I will be mortified if Paulo saw those stories. But before Amelia can go any further, Angela interrupts. "Girls, Girls!" she shouts, clapping her hands together. "Dinner is served." And I am so grateful for her pushy ways at this moment.

The waiters descend upon us with plates full of steak. There's so much meat around the table that I feel like we're at one of Julie's family pig-pickin's—and I wish I could teleport back to North Carolina this instant.

I spend the rest of the meal with my head down, which isn't hard because I'm concentrating on cutting my steak into tiny pieces and pushing them around my plate, taking a bite every few minutes. Amelia and Lucy flirt openly with Paulo, who doesn't seem to mind. I'm scared to even join in. Those girls have already bared their talons and shown that they are willing to go after me if I steal any attention from them, so I let it be. I'm sure Paulo is more interested in their type anyway—both are incredibly beautiful blondes of the Heidi Klum mold. And here I am with mousy hair and too many freckles, actually believing that a gorgeous Brazilian designer might be attracted to me. What a joke.

At the end of the night I stand up without even looking in Paulo's direction. I follow Angela out, giving Dona a quick kiss on the cheek as I see Angela do, and head back to the hotel. I'm so exhausted that I just sweep the gift bags off the bed into a pile, not worrying about wrinkled dresses or tangled jewelry, just wanting to fall into a deep sleep and forget the embarrassment of tonight.

four

I wake up to banging. The door? No, I realize as I open my eyes and stare at the filtered orange sunlight streaming through the window. It's my head.

Knock, knock, knock.

Okay, and the door. I am so not willing to face Angela at the inhuman hour of—I glance at the clock—six forty-three A.M.! She is losing it to try to get me up now. I know that the Dona Pink show isn't until four P.M.

Knock, knock, knock.

The woman is relentless. I stumble out from under my warm, cozy comforter and grab the hotel robe off the back of the bathroom door. At least it's fuzzy and soft to take some of the sting out of this morning.

I open the door, expecting to be blinded by Angela's so-gold-they're-almost-yellow highlights and gleaming veneers. Instead, I see dark smoky eyes, cheekbones from here to heaven, and bright red lips with a cigarette dangling from them.

"Veronica!"

"Hey, kid," says my old roommate, throwing her long, dark hair out of her face with a quick head toss. She pulls me in for a hug and although her arms are still bonier than most, I realize she looks about ten pounds heavier than she did all last spring. And that is definitely a *good* thing.

"Come in!" I say, more enthusiastically than I thought was possible at seven A.M. It's so great to see Veronica. Last year we had a gazillion ups and downs—we'd get close and then she'd push me away with caustic comments or disses in the press or a sabotaged go-see appointment to book a modeling job—but somehow I understood her. Maybe it's because we were (and are?) both insanely insecure.

We plop down on the bed and I throw off my robe and get under the covers again. Veronica spreads out along the other side of the king-size bed, her long legs dangling off the end. "Nice digs, Greenfield," she says, crushing her cigarette in the bedside ashtray. "You must have booked a lot of shows."

"Actually, just one," I say. "Dona Pink."

"Cool," she says. "Me too. I've also got Fraga and Vieira coming up. You never know, though. In Brazil, they can snag you last-minute without a run-through if they hear you're in town."

"Really?" I say.

"Oh yeah," says Veronica. "My first year I was originally booked for five shows, but I walked eleven. Anyway, Miss V, what's up with you?"

"Not that much," I say, feeling suddenly kind of shy. The last time I saw Veronica was in a rehab center in upstate New York. She was getting treatment for her drug use, and also trying to get over bulimia—not exactly a shopping-and-a-movie kind of friendship day. But we've been IMing all summer, and I know she's doing better now. At least I think she is. "Um, so how are you?" I ask.

"Oh, so we're going to use that worried tone when we talk about me?" asks Veronica, turning to face me.

"Oh, no. I mean, I didn't . . ." I start.

"It's okay," sighs Veronica. "Everyone does it. So, I haven't used any illegal drugs since the day you staged your own little intervention in the bathroom at our apartment, my weight is stabilized, and I have a healthy BMI—though I'm still not convinced that won't lose me some jobs."

"BMI?" I ask.

"Still a little sheltered, dear Violet?" says Veronica, smiling. "BMI stands for body mass index—it's only been in the news every other day for like two years. Basically, some countries are saying models are underweight and that they won't let you walk in their shows unless your BMI is a certain number. It has something to do with height and weight calculations. But whatever."

"Oh," I say, feeling silly for not having known. But Veronica isn't really making fun of me like she used to.

"So don't worry about me," she continues. "I'm staying away from bad influences like, oh, everyone I used to run with in New York."

"Except me!" I say, batting Veronica with an orange throw pillow.

"Yes, Miss Priss," she admits, laughing. "Except you."

Then my shyness fades and I find myself telling Veronica all about my summer at home with Julie and Roger—how Julie was dating my brother for a while but had to break it off before college, how the BK girls tiptoed around us at the pool because I finally stood up to them at prom last spring, and how my parents let me break curfew to drive with Julie and Roger to Carolina Beach. We parked the Rabbit on the sand and just stared at the sky all night.

"The three of you 'breaking curfew'?" asks Veronica, smirking and making air quotes. "Sounds utterly romantic."

"It's always been the three of us," I say, knowing that's cheesy but also feeling a rush of nostalgia for the summer that just happened.

"I'm just kidding, Mayberry," says Veronica. "I'm probably jealous because when I was your age, instead of having high school beach moments I was hanging out with tutors in between runway shows."

"You're like two years older than me," I shout, but then I look at her with sympathy. It probably *was* a sucky way to grow up. I mean, I can't even handle the modeling world rules at eighteen—my fourteen-year-old self would have been completely overwhelmed.

"Yeah, poor me," she says, standing up. "Man, I gotta pee."

While Veronica uses the fancy marble bathroom, I stand up and stretch. The phone rings and I look at the clock—still not even eight A.M.

"Vivid Violet." It's Angela.

"Morning, Angela," I say.

"Well, you do sound awake," she says, and I'm about to explain to her that Veronica's here and we've been catching up. But of course she has no time for those kinds of details. "Listen, darling, we've got to get you to the shows. Dona's is at four P.M. but a couple of other designers have asked about you and I want you on call just in case. Besides, you missed the run-through while you were galli-vanting around playing *Little House on the Prairie* or whatever you people in South Carolina do."

North, I think to myself, knowing it's pointless to correct Angela.

"So I'll meet you downstairs in ten minutes. Have a shower, dear, your hair was on the bad side of greasy last night. And tell Veronica I know she's here—the front desk confirmed her check-in. Drag her along with you when you come."

Dial tone. I really hate the way she never says good-bye. Isn't that just the basest of courtesies?

I'm expecting a field of white tents for the fashion show venues, like in New York, but instead I see a huge stadium looming in the cab's front window. My expression must give away my surprise, because suddenly Veronica says, "Welcome to Bienal—wait until you see the concrete floors."

The surrounding area, Ibirapuera Park, looks gorgeous—kind of like Central Park in New York with its trees and small ponds amid the São Paulo skyline. But the Fashion Week venue itself? Kind of blah.

We enter the Bienal Pavilion through a regular door, which seems to have members of the public flowing through it also. "So much for VIP life." Veronica sighs.

Angela shakes her head. "Try to be a little down-to-earth, Veronica," she says. "After all, this is your third strike moment."

I cringe inwardly—that was harsh. Veronica Trask used to be an incredibly huge name and face, like, three years ago, but she has had two stints in rehab now, and I know designers are backing off a little bit. Veronica confided in me over the summer that Kate Moss's comeback made her feel like she had always been B-list—and only A-listers can bounce back from scandals.

"Veronica Trask!" I hear a woman's voice yell from across the crowded easeway, and a kind of unattractive but really well-dressed woman runs over to air-kiss Veronica. "Amy," Veronica says, using her supersweet fake voice. "How are you?"

"Oh, good, good," says this Amy person. "Glad to be covering São Paulo again. Hey, you haven't been here in a while, right?"

"Don't remind me," says Veronica.

And then our ever-interrupting PR machine jumps in. "Veronica's rebuilding her image," says Angela. "She's had a challenging year."

Veronica and I roll our eyes at each other out of Angela's line of view. Her euphemisms are so annoying. It's like, why not just tell the truth? Everyone knows what code words like *rebuilding* and *challenging* mean. Sometimes I think agents are hired liars.

"And do I get an intro here?" asks Amy, changing the subject and gesturing toward me. Before Angela can go into her spiel about how

I took the summer off because I wanted to be fresh for fall shows (again, a total load of crap), Veronica steps in.

"I think you know she needs no intro, Amy," Veronica says. "This is Miss Violet Greenfield."

"Hi, Violet," says Amy, pumping my hand in a vigorous shake. "I did know it was you, but I wanted to make it formal. I'm Amy Stanhope, from the *New York Times*."

Oooh, I wish Roger could be here. I'm sure he'd know exactly where Amy Stanhope's byline has appeared over the last six months— he's kind of obsessed with reading the *Times* so he can feel smarter than everyone around him. He likes to say things like, "Well, yesterday in the *Times* . . ." and "You know, the *Times* says that . . ." almost apropos of nothing. And here I am shaking a *New York Times* writer's hand but not knowing a thing about her work. (And completely flattered that she knows who I am.)

"You know it caused a big hullabaloo last spring when you dropped the Voile campaign," she says.

Hullabaloo? I smile nervously at Amy, wondering how I can explain to her that the reason I left New York last year was because I had been broken down by the cold stares of fashion editors and model bookers, because I watched my roommate eat string beans every day and do coke in the bathroom every night, because my best friends at home were telling me I wasn't myself anymore, and because I was scared that I was becoming part of this soulless world that rewarded only the extremes of wild restriction and lavish excess. Probably not the best quote to give a *New York Times* reporter. As all this information flashes through my mind, I turn to Angela for help.

Before Angela can concoct some sort of excuse for why I would walk away from the biggest ad campaign of last year, Veronica jumps in and saves me in true superfriend style.

"Violet's a really smart girl," Veronica says, turning to Amy and practically body-blocking Angela. "She saw what I went through when fame hit me too fast, and she had to slow her own trajectory down a little bit. She wants to know who she is *before* she gives herself to the world."

Then Veronica reaches out and gives my hand a little squeeze. I feel like I'm going to tear up—that was *so* sweet. I wonder if she meant it. I kind of wish I could write it down, because even if that's not what I'm doing, it sounds like what I *should* be doing.

The answer seems to satisfy Amy, because she pulls out her pad and jots down some notes, then gives us a wave and says, "Off to the Zoomp show!"

Then Angela links her arm through Veronica's and says, "Have you thought about a career in PR?" before throwing her head back for a signature laugh. "Come on, my Double-V girls, let's go work some magic backstage."

five

After a couple hours of meeting various Brazilian designers who all seem to mill about backstage during the shows, I have come to the conclusion that I like it here. Although the language barrier makes it hard to get past "How are you?" and "You make beautiful clothes," everyone smiles, looks me in the eye, and really seems to care about what I'm trying to communicate.

"This place is like the polar opposite of New York," I whisper to Veronica as she snags a plastic champagne flute from the backstage stash of goodies, which includes just champagne and a trough of apples.

"Yeah," she says, grabbing an apple with her free hand. "There's even real food here! It's a limited selection, but it's edible." We lean back and giggle together.

"So, V," says Veronica. "I think you're a hit." She gestures at the chattering groups around us, and I suddenly notice that all of them seem to be surreptitiously glancing over at me and Veronica every few seconds.

"Why are they all looking at us?" I ask.

"They're looking at *you*," she says. "I heard Girola Calino and Karina Giotta fighting over whose show you'd do tomorrow."

"Really?" I ask, incredulous.

And then I see Angela bounding toward us with a Cheshire-cat grin on her face. "Violet, let's get you over to Dona's—the show is in a couple of hours," she says. "On the walk over we'll run through your schedule for tomorrow—you've got a few additional bookings."

I turn to Veronica, who smiles and gives me a little wave as she mouths, *Told you*. And while I wonder for a second if she's upset that I'm getting the bulk of the spotlight, I push the thought away quickly. This is a different Veronica from the one who screamed, "You will not take my place!" at me last year. I trust her.

On the way to Dona's dressing area, I feel the hairs on my arm start to prickle. I've been back in home mode for so long that I forgot how exciting a runway could be. A gorgeously punk-looking makeup artist applies a crazy green lightning bolt to my face while a pudgy, chattering hairstylist blows my hair into a faux-hawk. "David Bowie!" he shouts a few times, trying to communicate the inspiration for Dona's show in between his completely untranslatable chitchat. I wonder if he knows I don't understand him, but I just meet his eyes in the mirror and smile at whatever he says. I'm totally enjoying this.

When they're done, I have a Ziggy Stardust thing going on. Roger had a sixth-grade obsession with old David Bowie songs and made us listen to "The Rise and Fall of Ziggy Stardust and the Spiders from Mars" a million times—Julie and I dubbed it "weirdest title ever," but that was before emo bands started writing songs with twenty-word names.

I slip on a neon green bikini, which is the smallest thing I've ever worn in public, and I say a silent thank-you to Angela for forcing the issue on the waxing appointment. I guess there's a reason they're called *Brazilians*. As I hear the first strains of "Ziggy Stardust," I feel a strong longing for Roger to be here watching me, seeing what I do on the runway. I realize that all the butterflies from earlier are gone—I'm ready to be in the spotlight again.

I breathe deeply as I wait for my turn to walk, and I see *the* Graciella out of the corner of my eye. She has seven people crowding around her—I guess that's the supermodel treatment. She really is ethereal—long blond waves, perfectly tanned skin, and legs up to her neck. São Paulo is her hometown, so she always closes the shows she walks here. Suddenly I meet her eye and she smiles at me. So embarrassing that I'm staring, but she is really like a movie star— she's dated two big Hollywood actors. So far. I cannot believe Dona asked me to close the show with her.

I shake off the starstruck feeling because I have to remember the blocking instructions, especially since I missed the rehearsal by flying in late. The runway isn't a straight pier-style walk like in New York. This one is just an open floor, so the models are supposed to walk in a square, turning and pausing briefly at each of the four corners. There's no photographers' pit, just various shooters crouched near the front row.

When I hear my cue—which is a pretty sweet line, "Like some cat from Japan, he could lick 'em by smiling"—I step out in my high heels, and I can feel my back straighten and my chin lift as a hush falls over the crowd. *I wonder if they know who I am. Do they like American models? Hate them?* I'm feeling a positive vibe and I really love this song so I decide to pretend I'm famous. I'm back in full model stance, making each step deliberate as I do the "street" walk Dona wanted. It's kind of like the way people walk down a block in New York: strong, with no swish—that's for if you're modeling something with more fabric. At the end of the first corner, I stop and do a turn, catching flashbulbs and hoping they aren't picking up any flaws—these bikinis show off, like, every single inch of skin that's not blurrable on network TV.

As I approach the second corner, I'm focused on the turn marker (a little piece of tape on the ground). When I spin, I catch a smile that's half hidden by a flop of hair in the front row. Paulo. I feel my heart skip a beat and I break into what I'm sure is a huge, goofy grin just in time for the photographers to capture it on film. *I am a professional,* I think to myself as I keep walking, strong to the end. As soon as I get backstage, I let out a little sigh of joy. I swear I haven't had a crush this big since Brian Radcliff in high school. Which, okay, was just last year, but still.

To close the show, Graciella and I are both wearing pink neon polka-dot tops with yellow lightning-bolt bottoms. And I don't mean that the bottoms have a lightning design on them—I mean they're like two lightning bolts sewn together to form some semblance of a bikini bottom. It's more like a very thin V . . . right over my, uh, V.

I'm going to walk out hand in hand with one of the biggest supermodels in the world. Wearing what is essentially a V-string.

"Hello, Violet," says Graciella, leaning in to give me a double-cheek kiss.

"Hello," I say, realizing she's one of the only people I have to look up to. She must be six feet two. She turns to face the runway as we get ready to close the show, and I peek around her back. Full disclosure: I'm hoping to see some cellulite. Because if Graciella has cellulite, I will feel so much more okay with my own growth-induced stretch marks.

It's there! I mean, her butt is still epic, but she's a real person with jiggle, and I feel better for knowing that.

Then we get our cue, and I take her hand. She smiles at me and squeezes my fingers, and as we walk out it feels like a thousand flash-bulbs go off at once. I can hardly see as we clomp down the runway together. Me and Graciella.

I am *so* not in Carolina anymore.

After the show is over, Graciella gives me a big "Mwah!" kiss on the lips and tells me I made her look good. As if. Then she smiles and scoots rapidly off to her fabulous life, seven groupies in tow.

As I'm wiping off my makeup, Veronica finds me backstage and pops open a bottle of champagne, spraying me with the explosive foam.

"Hey! No fair!" I shout, laughing.

"Totally fair," she says. "You're wearing a bathing suit!"

Angela runs over to us and holds out her glass for a toast. I'm feeling so elated that I actually pull her in for a hug. Then we raise our plastic glasses.

"To Brazil!" I say.

"To Violet!" says Veronica.

"To the runway!" adds Angela, just as we attempt to clink our synthetic flutes together.

Because there's still a goody-goody inside of me, I justify drinking partly by the fact that I'm totally legal here at eighteen, but as I sip my second bubbly drink of the day, I remember what was intoxicating about this world. And I start to forget why I left it last year.

six

Back at the hotel, I finally get my wireless connection working. I'm a little bit tipsy when I log on, but I immediately start a chat with Julie and Roger, a.k.a. Diane Sawyer (because Julie is such a wannabe journalism superstar) and RC1 (for Rivers Cuomo, hipster idol).

VIOLET GREENFIELD: hola!
RC1: Wait—is this the *real* Violet Greenfield?

Roger always uses perfect punctuation on IM—it's one of his "smarter than you" tactics, and it makes me smile.

VIOLET GREENFIELD: duh, yes
RC1: Prove it.
RC1: What mind-boggling question did Richard ask you to help you land the movie theater job the day you turned sixteen?

VIOLET GREENFIELD: if you saw a piece of popcorn on the floor, what would you do?

DIANE SAWYER: pick it up!!!

VIOLET GREENFIELD: jules!

RC1: Trivia interference!

DIANE SAWYER: enough testing rivers

DIANE SAWYER: v did you meet graciella?

VIOLET GREENFIELD: y! walked the runway with her like 2 hours ago

RC1: Is she single? Perhaps looking for an intellectual Superman type about four years her junior?

DIANE SAWYER: more like a clark kent without the superman gene

VIOLET GREENFIELD: dream on, roger!

Then there's a knock at my door.

VIOLET GREENFIELD: gotta go you guys

VIOLET GREENFIELD: more later

VIOLET GREENFIELD: xoxoxoxo

I log off and run to the door. I wanted to tell Julie about Paulo-the-pettable, but Veronica and I are going to a celebratory dinner together tonight. Angela wanted us to go out with the Tryst girls, but Veronica was like, "No way," and Angela actually said okay. Well, after Veronica spun some magic about wanting to coach me for tomorrow's shows.

I fling open the door and scream, "Hey, supermodel!"

But it's not Veronica. It's Paulo. And I haven't even brushed my hair or washed my face fully since the Dona show. A wave of mortification washes over me as I stutter, "Oh, um, Paulo. I thought it was . . . um, want to come in?"

Why am I inviting him into my hotel room? It's messy with gift bags that I went through like a five-year-old on Christmas morning and there's dirty underwear in the corner!

"Oh, no," says Paulo, smiling sweetly and showing off these amazing white teeth with a gap in the center that is so sexy I think I might faint. "I just . . . brought you these." He holds out a bunch of yellow daisies, and my heart starts pounding as I hear two distinct voices in my head start to immediately analyze the situation.

Giddy voice: *Does he like me?*
Downer voice: *Of course not. This must be a common courtesy in Brazil, designer to model.*
Giddy: *Not if you're not in his show. He totally likes me! He like likes me.*
Downer: *Quiet! You're going to get all red and flustered.*

"Thank you," I say. "They're beautiful."

"Ah, no," whispers Paulo. "That is a word for you, not silly flowers."

Giddy: *See!*

I smile and blush, not sure what to say.

"I would very much like you to be in my show," says Paulo. "It is two days from now. Are you free?"

"Yes," I say, despite the fact that I have no knowledge of my schedule. I'll make time.

"Good," says Paulo, touching my chin with his soft fingers and leaning in to kiss my ever-reddening cheek with his amazingly full lips. "I will see you soon."

Then he's gone. I close the door and lean against it to catch my breath, sliding down to the floor and clutching the daisies to my chest. I let out the kind of audible sigh you can only really indulge in when you're completely alone. Giddy won that round. I'm completely smitten.

The next day is a total blur. Veronica had rolled her eyes when I told her about Paulo's flowers-behind-the-back charm, but she did help me go over some designer knowledge at dinner last night. Like Isabela always makes sweet, girly lines and Alexandre does themed looks—this year's collection has a Spanish matador influence. I keep hearing fashion editors walking around backstage saying things like, "Wasn't that reminiscent of Marc in 2004?" I mean, how do they keep this stuff in their heads? I'm learning how important it is, though, so I'm trying to catch up.

After walking two runways, I am back in my runway groove but still totally nervous about Paulo's show. I really want to be great for him. His clothes are lovely—all soft and romantic, but with really defined shapes—like tight versions of peasant blouses and long skirts, but not in a dorky medieval-reenactor costume kind of way. He makes things look modern with unexpected colors and fabrics (that's what Veronica says when she's trying to sound like a fashion writer). I'm wearing a brocaded silver bustier with a stick-straight skirt that goes down to my calves, and I have only one walk, Paulo told me. I wonder if he thinks I'm not good enough to go out twice, but I'm really trying not to let my insecure thoughts take over. This is the new Violet on the runway—totally confident and cool. I hope.

The night before Paulo's show, I'm intent on going to bed kind of early so I'll be awake and de-eye-bagged tomorrow. Then the phone rings. I look at the clock—midnight.

"Hello?"

"Violet?" says a gorgeous voice. It's Paulo!

"Paulo?"

"Did I wake you?"

"No, I was just, um, getting ready to go out."

I don't want to sound like a loser, and I know the other Tryst girls are partying tonight. Earlier, even Veronica sighed, "Okay, lame-o," when I told her I didn't want to hit the São Paulo incarnation of Marquee, a New York nightclub I'm all too familiar with.

"How about going somewhere with me?" says Paulo, bringing me back to the present, where there is a much hotter guy than last year's Peter Heller asking me out right now. I think.

"Oh," I say, feeling my whole body break into a grin. "Okay."

"It's for work," says Paulo, and I can feel my grin fading. "To show you the runway. I'll pick you up in ten minutes."

"Great," I say, putting on my all-business voice. "I'll be ready."

When I hang up, I'm confused. Did Paulo just ask me out, or did he just schedule a business meeting for midnight?

I throw on some tight jeans and my can't-miss Prada boots, along with a full-coverage black turtleneck sweater that my mom made me pack. If this isn't a date, I don't want to look all trying-too-hard.

When Paulo leads me out to his car, I can't help but laugh. It's this sputtering, black-and-gray antiquey-looking car with circular headlights.

"Violet, meet Gracie," he says, holding the passenger-side door open for me.

"Hello, Gracie," I say, sliding onto her black leather seats. There is a stick shift the size of a pool cue between us, but Paulo handles it gently as we drive toward the stadium.

"Gracie is my first love," says Paulo, staring ahead as he talks to me in a low, sweet voice about how he found the car rusting in a garage near his family's country home and brought "her" back to life. As I watch the bouncing city lights pass through these tiny, manual roll-up windows, I feel like I'm in a classic old movie. I don't say much; I'm just listening to Paulo talk, and I get up the confidence to believe that this is *totally* a date.

When we arrive at the stadium, Paulo takes out a huge ring of keys and opens a back entrance. "Designer perk," he says, holding the door open for me and smiling. We walk down a long hallway. "You know my show is only six minutes," says Paulo, turning to me and smiling. "That's why you're only walking once. Everybody's walking once."

"Oh, I didn't think . . ." I start.

"It's *okay*, Violet," interrupts Paulo. "I just wanted you to know why. I have a small—but very distinctive—collection."

I smile at him in what I hope is a casual way, but inside I'm so relieved! The show is *short*—usually they go like fifteen minutes—that's why I'm only walking once. Thank God it's not because he thinks I'm not good enough.

We're heading toward a set of heavy black curtains. When we reach them, Paulo has to struggle to pull back one side of the weighted fabric and let me into the runway area.

As soon as the curtain opens, I'm bathed in blue light. I feel a shiver run through me. The Bienal Pavilion may be a little downscale, but the artistry of São Paulo Fashion Week is winning me over. This is no ordinary runway.

"Ice," whispers Paulo in a cloud of frosty breath.

The runway, which is a red carpet, weaves through giant blocks of ice. Like ice cubes, but each taller than I am, and stacked on top of each other three levels high.

"I've been dreaming of ice castles since I was five years old," says Paulo. "Maybe because we have no real winter in São Paulo."

"It's beautiful," I say softly, entranced by the way the lights reflect off the shiny ice surface.

"I'm glad you like it," says Paulo, taking my hand. "I wanted to have something different, something exotic. And you are the perfect exotic girl to close the show."

I look at him questioningly. *Me? Exotic?* Well, I guess I *am* foreign here. It's so weird to think of myself as foreign. Paulo's foreign. Not me.

"Um . . . thanks," I say, suddenly coming out of my trance and realizing I'm in an oversized meat locker with a guy I barely know. If Paulo wanted to kill me, he could keep me fresh for weeks before anyone smelled anything. *Stop*—why is my train of thought going there? Sometimes I wonder if I'm crazy. A look back at Paulo's soft lips gets me right back into fantasy zone.

"I thought you might practice your walk," he says. "You missed the rehearsal, and the course is a little . . . tricky."

I nod, and he grabs a pair of red lace-up ankle boots from the corner—the ones I'll wear in the show. The heel must be four inches. I pull off my shoes and Paulo helps me lace up.

As he leads me down the red carpet, we turn left, then right and right again, making a square figure-eight walk through the ice. We're totally silent as we walk, and I'm thinking about how glad I am the runway *itself* isn't ice—I'm having enough trouble in these heels. When we get back to the starting point, Paulo says, "Perfect."

My thoughts exactly.

seven

       I got about four hours of sleep. After Paulo and I finished "practice," he drove me back to the hotel and gave me a sweet—if not passionate—kiss on the lips. I almost went in for more, but then I realized he wasn't actually going for a make-out session in his antique car while the bellhop was waiting for me.

Now I'm in a chair, getting makeup done for Paulo's show and hoping it'll hide the bags under my eyes. I don't want to have to tell Veronica about last night. Not yet. I want to keep it for me.

Suddenly, I hear a familiar Australian accent behind me. I turn into the green mascara wand—"oops, sorry!" I say to my makeup lady, who rolls her eyes—but I'm so distracted I forget to feel rude.

"Sam!" I yell, hopping out of the makeup chair to hug my former New York roommate, the third and final tenant of our agency-sponsored Tryst model apartment last year.

"V!" she screams, her red curls bouncing. "I heard you were here! I had to come watch your international debut—and get in a little nightlife with my girl."

"You flew all the way to Brazil to see me?" I ask.

"Don't be silly," says Veronica, who's walking up behind Sam. "She was in Rio. Right, Sam?"

"Veronica," says Sam, looking not completely happy to see our third roommate. The two of them never really did get along, and I feel torn because Veronica and I have gotten close, but last year Sam was the one who really gave me the dirt on how things worked in the modeling industry . . . Veronica was just sulky and insulting most of the time. But that was before rehab and before I really understood where her anger and angst came from. Still, seeing the narrowed eyes Veronica has positioned on Sam, I recall traces of the intimidating girl I met last year—the one who could make me cry with a sideways glance.

"It's true," says Sam, dropping her frown and turning to me with a smile. "I was in Rio doing Fashion Week, but I wanted to come party with you!"

"It's so great to see you, Sam," I say, and I really mean it.

"You too, V," she says. "Now get back to makeup. I'll play audience member outside—Paulo got me a second-row seat."

"Still not A-list enough for front row, Sam?" sneers Veronica. "Aw. That's sad."

Sam just waves at me and bounds out of the backstage area, ignoring Veronica. I, on the other hand, am annoyed.

"Why do you have to be like that?" I say to Veronica, stomping back to my chair and sitting for the thoroughly exasperated makeup woman, who will probably screw up my face on purpose now that I've held her up for so long. "Sorry," I whisper to her, trying to give her my sincerest eyes. She grunts, not buying it.

"Be like what?" says Veronica, following me to my chair. "It's not like Sam is really your friend, Violet. Don't be naïve."

"What do you mean?" I ask.

"I mean she's been clinging to your coattails since day one, looking for any chance to get a piece of what you have," says Veronica.

"That's not true!" I shout. "I'm not listening to you."

"Fine," says Veronica. "Have it your way. I'm just trying to protect you, Miss North Carolina." Then she storms off, leaving me wondering who to trust. I hate this feeling. I hate that Veronica can plant this doubt in my head. Why can't people just be normal?

As if on cue, Angela rushes over to me in my makeup chair, panting about my spot in Paulo's show. She is *so* not normal.

"You're the closer," she says.

"I know," I say, hopping out of the chair and smiling at the makeup lady, who still totally hates me. I take two deep breaths. "I'm ready."

I'm so glad I practiced the figure-eight walk—it's kind of confusing. There's this amazing Brazilian music playing in the background. There aren't any words, just tinkling noises. Not like pee tinkle, but like bell tinkle. It really goes well with the ice effect.

When I march off the runway, I hear uproarious applause, and I get ready to go out for the final walk, when all the models go out in a row to give the crowd one more look at the collection and let the designer take a bow.

Paulo grabs my hand. "We go together," he says, and before I can respond, we're back out in the spotlight, smiling for photographers who snap us holding hands as we walk past. When we get to the top of the figure-eight formation, Paulo pauses. I'm not sure how to react, so I begin to pull away—he must be getting ready to take a bow up here, on center stage. The other models have hustled off the runway, but Paulo holds fast to my hand.

Then, like Patrick Swayze showing Jennifer Grey ballroom dancing techniques in that classic *Dirty Dancing* movie, Paulo pulls my arm and firmly spins my body into his. He leans me back for a dip and kisses me right on the lips. But this isn't a kiss like last night's quick good-bye. This is a long, luxurious, take-me-now kind of kiss.

One that makes my knees shake like Jell-O, my arms flop like boiled spaghetti. After what seems like an hour, I realize that I'm upright again, marching off the runway at Paulo's heels.

I swear my eyes can't focus for at least twenty minutes.

"What was *that*?" screams Veronica as I open my hotel room door. I'm wearing just the hotel bathrobe. I've been soaking in a bubble bath for half an hour, replaying what will now and forever be known as The Kiss in my head and waiting for Julie's IM icon to pop up so I can dish.

"What?" I say, smiling coyly. Paulo invited me to a party at his house tonight, and I am truly hoping for The Kiss, Act II.

"Violet Greenfield, you are getting yourself in big trouble!" shouts Veronica. And I realize that she's not treating this in a best-friend way where we get to analyze it for hours—the firm-but-sexy way he turned me toward him, the feel of his lips on mine, how his strong arms supported my weight as I went into full-swoon mode. She's truly angry.

"Oh, please, Veronica," I say, rolling my eyes and sitting down on my bed. "It was just a kiss." I guess I'd better downplay things if she's going to get all psycho.

"It was a PR stunt, Greenfield," she says, leaning against the wall and folding her arms across her chest. "But I could tell by your deer-in-headlights face at the end that you did not recognize that fact."

"It didn't feel like a stunt to me," I say softly, bunching up little bits of the comforter between my hands. I never know how to handle it when people yell and get aggro with me—it's completely uncomfortable. I wish Veronica would calm down.

"Did it not feel like there were a thousand cameras up in your face?" says Veronica.

"Actually, no," I say, realizing that the flashes I saw might not have been solely due to fireworks of lust.

"Well there *were*," she huffs. "Wake up, Violet. This is all for publicity for Paulo's line, which—let me say—left a lot to be desired. A six-minute show? He must be crazy. He's just a spoiled rich kid with no talent!"

At that moment, I realize something: Veronica is *still* jealous. She's jealous of my friendship with Sam, she's jealous that I'm walking more shows than she is, and she's jealous of what's going on with Paulo. I don't care what she says—I know that that kiss was more than a PR stunt.

"I'd like you to leave," I hear myself say in a calm voice that sounds surprisingly authoritative.

"What?" says Veronica, taken off guard.

"Please go," I say. "You're being really mean, and you don't know what you're talking about."

"Violet, I'm just trying to—" Veronica starts.

"Protect me?" I finish for her. "Like last year when you made out with Peter while I was dating him? Like when you told the *Post* I was a dumb little virgin from the sticks who'd never make it in New York?"

"That's not fair," says Veronica. "I was a different person—in a really bad place. We're friends now—I want to help you."

"Oh, sure," I say sarcastically. "I'm not as naïve as I was back then, Veronica."

She looks at me long and hard before she turns and heads for the door. Before she closes it, she looks back at me. "But you're still a virgin," she says, matter-of-factly. So much for trusting new friends.

eight

As I get into a limo with Sam, I try to push the confrontation with Veronica out of my head. I don't even bring it up with Sam, because I feel like it'll be fuel for her hatred of Veronica, and I'm not sure how I feel about everything yet.

"Shall we?" asks Sam, pulling a bottle of champagne from the built-in fridge. Paulo sent the limo to pick us up because he's busy getting ready for the party, which is at his mansion in the chic Vila Madalena neighborhood.

"Definitely!" I say, wanting to forget about things for the night and just have fun.

"That was *some* kiss this afternoon," says Sam.

"I know!" I squeal, unable to hold back. "It was awesome—I truly felt like my feet had left the ground."

"Yeah, that's what a kiss from Paulo will do," says Sam.

I eye her suspiciously.

"Or so I hear!" she says, laughing.

I'm still staring at her warily.

"Seriously, Violet," she says. "I'm kidding! I don't even know Paulo. I've just heard he's quite a lip-locker."

"Really?" I ask, afraid to hear more but wanting to.

"Oh, it doesn't matter," says Sam. "Word on the street is he's only got his eye on one girl these days."

"Oh," I say, slumping back into my seat. I'm so lame for getting excited. Paulo probably kisses every model he closes the show with, like every year. But I have to ask. "Who is she?"

"You, dork!" shouts Sam, clinking her glass with mine.

Me?! I smile and down my champagne.

Paulo's house is behind this huge iron gate, set back in a gorgeously manicured lawn with bushes shaped like cones and tropical fruit trees, which just make Paulo himself seem more romantic, if only for living in this cinematic setting.

When Sam and I walk into the large foyer, I know we look good. I'm wearing a gray-and-red striped bustier top and long, skinny cigarette pants that balance out the major décolletage show. Oh, and bright red heels. I feel like Audrey Hepburn in some old movie—like I should be riding around Rome on a scooter. Sam looks equally chic in an ivory-colored eyelet lace sundress that shows off her freckled shoulders and pale, glowing skin.

"Let's go," she says, linking arms with me as we follow the butler—hello! *butler!*—out to the pool area. Dozens of beautiful people are smiling, chatting, throwing their heads back in exaggerated but graceful laughter. I see a few faces turn our way, and I start to feel shy. Which means I need another champagne. Tonight I am determined not to be Violet Greenfield, high school wallflower. I am Violet Greenfield, international runway star and irresistible temptress. Or something.

I steer Sam toward the bar area, which features a champagne fountain surrounded by bowls and bowls of strawberries. As I'm leaning over to catch a stream of champagne in my glass, I feel a hand on my back and I see a strawberry near my mouth. Without hesitation, I bite into it. When I turn around, Paulo kisses me on the lips and says, "Mmm . . ." as we part. I smile as I see Sam shuffle away from the corner of my eye. She's a good wingman—she knows when to step back.

"When do you leave?" asks Paulo, looking at me with intense eyes.

"Two days," I say, suddenly realizing that I don't want to leave. Not even a little bit.

"You have more shows?" says Paulo.

"I'm not sure," I say. "I mean, Angela probably wants me to . . ."

"Because I have to ask you something," Paulo interrupts. "My line is finally ready for a full-scale ad campaign. And I want Violet Greenfield to be the face of Paulo Forte."

"You do?" I ask, feeling dizzy as I take in the candles by the pool, the sky full of stars above our heads, and Paulo's hopeful face.

"Yes," says Paulo. "The shoot will take two weeks at the most. We aren't Chanel, but we can pay you something, and I can provide you with accommodations too, so that Tryst won't have any expenses. Say you will, Violet. You're the only girl I'll have."

And what else could I possibly do? "I will," I hear myself say.

"What are you guys talking about?" says a bubbly voice. Sam reaches over to refill her champagne glass. "Sorry to interrupt, but I need another drink."

"Not at all, Samantha," says Paulo, smiling. "Violet has just agreed to be the face of Paulo Forte for our very first national ad campaign."

"Really?!" says Sam. "Violet, that's great!" She reaches over to hug me, and I am in shock. I mean, it's cool about the campaign, but all I can think is, *Paulo wants me to stay in Brazil.* I am dying.

"Everyone, everyone!" shouts Paulo, clinking a spoon against his crystal champagne flute. *Uh-oh.*

When the crowd quiets, Paulo starts to rattle off some speech in Portuguese that is—judging by the crowd's reaction—both hilarious

and filled with good news. I'm hoping it's about how he's glad everyone came to the party, how he trusts the champagne fountain will
flow for the rest of the evening, how he wants Brazil to do well in
the World Cup . . . but the way he keeps gesturing to me makes me
feel like, somehow, the speech is about more than that. I try to smile
casually, but I'm sure I have that scared, wide-eyed Cupie doll look
on my face.

When Paulo's done, after the applause dies down, he repeats
himself in English: "I'd like to announce that Miss Violet Greenfield, who needs no introduction, will do me the honor of appearing
in my first national advertising campaign, to be shot in the coming
weeks in Brazil. Everyone, please, welcome Violet to our city and to
our hearts."

I scan the crowd for Angela. I assumed she'd be at the party but I
don't see her. Phew. At least I have twelve hours to think of a way to
tell her what happened.

Another round of clapping and a few congratulatory cheek kisses
later, I'm feeling a little shaky. Sam and I grab a cab and head back to
the hotel. I did get one more amazing smooch from Paulo as he put
us in the car and said, "See you soon, my muse." And although I really want to linger in this moment and replay those kisses in my head
while I listen to Coldplay in my room, I have a feeling that, like
Veronica warned, I've gotten myself in trouble.

"What did I just do?" I ask Sam.

She looks at me with her brow furrowed. "Well, V," she says.
"You just agreed to a Brazilian fashion campaign without the con-
sent of your agent, your parents, or your old roommate."

I let a little "eek" escape me.

"'Eek' is right," says Sam.

Brrring-brring. My hotel phone double-rings at six twelve
A.M. This can't be good.

"I'm on my way to the hotel, Violet!" shouts Angela. "And you'd better have a good explanation for the early edition of *O Estado de São Paulo*."

"Is that a newspaper?" I ask, but she's gone. The preemptive hangup is nothing unusual, but the fact that she didn't insert a V-adjective in front of my name makes me fear that Angela is extremely pissed.

I stumble out of bed and pull on my new favorite outfit, a.k.a. the hotel robe. Outside my door, the *O Estado* newspaper stares up at me accusingly. Luckily, I'm not on the front page. But as I spread it out on the bed, I realize there's a whole section that covers Fashion Week—and I'm *all over it*. Me in the lightning-bolt bikini, me drinking champagne with Veronica backstage, me walking in front of the glowing blue ice blocks. But more than just photos of me, there are photos of me and Paulo. Kissing on the runway at his show (there are three angles of that one), feeding each other strawberries (in the light of day that seems completely cheesy) and lip-locked by the champagne fountain (again, a tad cheesy, my morning self admits).

The main photo, though, is of me with the scared Cupie-doll face, standing alongside Paulo, who has his champagne flute raised in the air. The headline reads, "Violet Greenfield is the new face of Paulo Forte," and the subhead says, "American model steals Brazilian spotlight, designer's heart." I always hate it when they have to fit a line of words and don't have room to write things out fully, but after years of dealing with Julie on the high school newspaper staff, I know that the subhead is basically implying that I've got not only the attention of the country, but also Paulo's love—or at least a media-hyped crush. And before I can help myself, I smile.

My brief joy is interrupted by thunderous knocking. Angela. I open the door to face the most rumpled version of my agent I've yet seen. Her hair is tousled, her sunglasses are crooked, and she's without lipstick, which is completely unprecedented.

"What do you have to say for yourself?!" she demands, shaking the newspaper at me.

"There's no such thing as bad publicity?" I shrug, giving her my most innocent, Carolina smile.

"Violet Greenfield, how dare you accept a job without consulting me! Let alone allowing a public announcement of it at a party with media in attendance!"

"Well, I didn't really . . ." I start.

"I don't want to hear it!" she screams. "This is not what you came here to do—get charmed by some two-bit designer and end up staying in Brazil when you should be making connections for fall shows. I need you to *focus*."

"Well, I thought it would be good for me," I say, trying to think of ways to make Angela stop yelling. I so hate it when people yell. "I mean, it's a national campaign and I thought—"

"A national campaign *in Brazil!*" shouts Angela, still yelling, but losing momentum, I can tell. "This is small-time, Violet. You have to start thinking bigger. You could have a real career in front of you, but not if you drop to your knees every time a cute boy bats his eyes at you."

"That's not—" I start again. But it's no use trying to talk.

"Oh, please!" says Angela, almost down to inside-voice level. "Anyone can see you're smitten with the little bastard."

And then I see the corners of her mouth turn up—just briefly. It was a flash moment, but I caught it. And I realize that as mad as Angela is, she's also going to let me stay. She's going to let me do Paulo's campaign.

"But now that it's been announced publicly," she says, "I suppose we'll have to honor the commitment."

I break into a huge grin.

"But don't think I'm happy about it!" she snaps, all business again. "Two weeks, Vexing Violet. Then I want you back in the States getting prepped for the European shows."

I nod my head vigorously.

"Who knows?" says Angela, turning toward the door. "A little international romance could mature your reputation a bit."

Then she turns back to me and points her finger in a scolding-teacher way. "I'll call your mother and tell her you'll be staying longer," she says. "Wait until tomorrow to talk to your parents."

"Okay," I say as I move to shut the door behind her. Then I peek my head out as she's walking down the hall. "Angela?" I say. "Thanks."

Without slowing, she raises her perfectly manicured hand in a dismissive, fluttering wave. Then she's gone.

And I've bought myself two more weeks with Paulo.

nine

"Good lord, Violet, what do you have in these things?" Paulo laughs. He's carrying my luggage up the three wide steps to the pool house behind his mansion.

"The gift bag swag made my suitcases heavier," I say, smiling. "I swear!"

When Paulo said he would arrange a living situation for me while I was here, I pictured a hotel, or maybe even a model apartment with a few girls like when I lived in New York. What I didn't bet on—and what I conveniently left out when I talked to my parents last night—was that I'd be staying in Paulo's pool house. It's actually a gorgeous spot—a studio with huge windows that sit just above the outdoor hot tub. There's a tiny kitchen and bathroom, plus a big living area with a couch that folds into a bed. What more could a girl need?

And . . . well, it's near Paulo.

"I'll let you get settled in," Paulo says, kissing my hand as he walks backward down the steps and back to his house.

"See you at eight!" I yell, too loudly and doofily. We're supposed to have dinner tonight with the photographer who's shooting Paulo's campaign. We have to start working tomorrow.

I fall back onto the fluffy white bed with a happy sigh. As my eyelids get heavier, I pull the comforter up over my shoulder and drift off for a nap.

When I wake up, it's almost eight. Before I shower, I flip over and turn on my laptop, hoping I can catch Julie and Roger. Even though these next two weeks are going to be a dream, it's like they're almost not real until I get to talk to my friends about what's going on. Sam was excited for me, and she stopped by before she flew back to New York. Veronica didn't call, but then I didn't call her either. I almost did, but I was too afraid she would try to bring me down again.

When I log on to IM, Julie's not there, but Roger is.

VIOLET GREENFIELD: roger!

RC1: Miss Brazil. How is the land of the bare waxes?

VIOLET GREENFIELD: ugh—don't bring that up!

RC1: You didn't!

VIOLET GREENFIELD: well . . .

RC1: I'm blushing. Next topic: You're flying back tomorrow, right?

VIOLET GREENFIELD: nope. staying to do a campaign

RC1: Oh. For how long?

VIOLET GREENFIELD: a couple of weeks. so excited!! it's for paulo forte and he is so cute

Pause.

VIOLET GREENFIELD: i'm even staying at his pool house!!

I'm waiting so long that I think RC1 is about to go idle.

VIOLET GREENFIELD: rog?

RC1: You'd better IM Julie for girl talk.

VIOLET GREENFIELD: what's that supposed to mean?

RC1: I'm not your BFF, Violet. I'm a guy. Save the "so cute!!!!" nonsense.

VIOLET GREENFIELD: wtf?

RC1: Just make sure your little boy toy isn't a replica of that douchebag who screwed you over last year.

VIOLET GREENFIELD: oh shut up. this is different

RC1: I hope so. Because good old Roger might not be around this time to pick up the pieces if you get your heart broken.

RC1 has logged off.

How did that conversation spiral out of control? I briefly wonder if my brother somehow logged in as Roger and IMed with me like that as a prank, but then I remember that Roger has this super password with a crazy numbers-and-letters combination that he never tells anyone because he's neurotic like that.

"Knock, knock." Paulo's adorable accent breaks my confusion. Roger's probably just in a bad mood.

"Ready?" asks Paulo, raising an eyebrow as he looks down at me. I'm still in my sweats and T-shirt.

"Oh! I fell asleep and then I was IMing with my friend, who's acting really weird—" I start. I'm rambling. Horribly.

"Violet, Violet, slow down," says Paulo, smiling. "I'll wait." Then he sits on the edge of the bed.

I stare back at him for a second and then jump out of bed, determined to be ready in less than three minutes. I throw open my red suitcase and grab the long-sleeved black wrap dress that never wrinkles, a pair of black heels, and my toiletry bag. Then I run for the bathroom and get dressed, pulling my hair up into a messy bun and quickly applying blue mascara and red lip stain. I spritz myself with

Vichy water, which makes my face feel fresh and dewy and I'm ready to go.

When I step out of the bathroom, Paulo starts clapping. "Two minutes, thirty seconds," he says. "I'm impressed. And you look gorgeous."

"Thank you," I say, pleased with myself. I take his arm and we head toward the garage, where Gracie, the car, is waiting to take us into the lights of São Paulo.

Over the next few days, I feel like I'm living in a movie. Paulo keeps saying how much work there is to be done, but it turns out this "work" involves scouting locations for the campaign shoot. So far, we've gone down to Rio to sail on a millionaire's luxury yacht, had two picnics on the beach—one at sunrise and one at sunset, to gauge the lighting—and toured the private homes of São Paulo's wealthiest citizens. We even spent a day shopping on Rua Oscar Freire, the Rodeo Drive of São Paulo, to see what an "urban chic" background would be like.

By the end of the week, I'm giddily exhausted, and Paulo declares a day of rest before we start shooting. I'm sitting by the side of his aqua blue pool, bundled up in yoga pants and a hoodie, yes, but still really enjoying the late-morning winter sun. I look around at my little guest house, the tropical plants at the edge of the pool area, the soft lounge chairs that are a gajillion times nicer than my neighborhood swim club's plastic-slatted seats. I can't help but imagine myself as a character on *The O.C.* or *Beverly Hills 90210.* Paulo let me hook my iPod up to his outdoor stereo speakers, which are hidden among the plants on the grounds, so everyone on the estate today is listening to a mix of the Fray, the Killers, and Rihanna.

I breathe in, trying to save this moment. Sometimes, if I'm really aware that something amazing is happening in the present, I can will myself to make a photographic memory of a setting and a feeling—like once in sixth grade when I was in a car with Julie and Roger and that old eighties song "Eternal Flame" came on. For some reason, we all knew the words and just started spontaneously singing it together, that kind of singing where you're really passionate and into the words. I imprinted that memory in my mind, and I realized I had the power to remember a moment if I really tried.

Paulo comes walking down the path from the main house, looking adorable in a soft white button-down shirt, which is half open despite the chilly air, and tight blue jeans. Somehow foreign guys and hipsters can pull off the tightest pants ever. I smile as I imagine Roger wearing pants that snug—he probably will at NYU this year.

"What's that smile?" asks Paulo, as he sits down next to me.

"Oh, nothing," I say, turning to give him a kiss on the cheek. We haven't gone a day without a major make-out session—on the aforementioned yacht, beaches, and mansion grounds—and I'm starting to wonder how much longer I'll be able to stand saying good-bye to him at midnight and falling asleep alone. I've gone further with Paulo than I ever did with Peter Heller last year—but I'm still not sure I'm ready to go all the way. Sometimes I feel like the last eighteen-year-old virgin on earth, but Julie hasn't played her V-card yet either, which makes me feel less lame.

"So . . . ?" I say expectantly. I still don't know which location Paulo's chosen for the photo shoot, but he promised to make a decision by today.

He laughs out loud. "Patience, Violet," he says, grabbing my hand. "Will you do me the honor of accompanying me to dinner tonight? All will be revealed."

"Well, if all will be revealed, then I guess I can free up my schedule," I say. I kind of love how comfortable I've gotten with Paulo. I can flirt and be myself, I can tease him unself-consciously, we can kiss without my face turning cherry red—it's great.

"Oh, well, thank you for being flexible," says Paulo, leaning in for another kiss. After a few smooches, he stands up to go. "I really did mean today was for rest," he says. "So I'm leaving you to enjoy the pool and your magazines and whatever you like. If you need anything, call star-zero on the phone and someone will fetch it for you. I'll be back around seven P.M. to take you to dinner. Think casual."

I smile and nod, watching Paulo walk back toward the house.

"Oh!" he says, suddenly, turning around. "You got a letter today." He walks back to me, pulling an envelope out of his pocket.

"I did?" I ask, surprised. I didn't give anyone the address here. I glance at the return address. *Roger*.

"Thanks," I say, setting down the envelope and waiting until Paulo's figure is completely out of sight before tearing it open.

Dearest Violet, it starts.

ten

After I've read the letter from Roger a few times, I fold it and stick it in my hoodie pocket with a sigh. I realize I read it so many times that I've memorized it:

Dearest Violet,

In the tradition of kings and queens—and everyone in those Jane Austen books you love—I decided to sit down with pen and paper to draft our formal good-bye. Because you have chosen to stay in Brazil, I will not be seeing you again. I signed up for an early orientation at NYU, and I will be gone when you return to Chapel Hill. Despite our recent confrontation over IM, I want you to know that as you try to find yourself in the precarious world of skeletal fashionistas and beauty-hungry boy-toys, I will always be within shouting distance, always ready to rush to your aid, always there in case you need me. Always, Your Roger.

I notice that his handwriting is incredibly neat, which means he probably took his painstaking time writing the note—Roger's natural scrawl is pretty illegible. His tone is incredibly formal, but that is *so* Roger. Someday he will be the most old-fashioned, chivalrous boyfriend, probably for an NYU girl who doesn't deserve him. As I run my fingers over the smooth paper in my pocket and stare into the blue water of Paulo's pool, my iPod shuffles into an old-school Smiths song, "Please, Please, Please Let Me Get What I Want."

Later that afternoon, post–hot shower and magazine reading time and an amazing steak sandwich that Paulo's butler Elvis brought me for lunch, I log on to IM. I *need* to talk to Julie, and thank God she's online.

VIOLET GREENFIELD: hey!
DIANE SAWYER: hey, vi!
VIOLET GREENFIELD: what's up?
DIANE SAWYER: about to go meet jake. we're having total angst over me leaving
DIANE SAWYER: so painful!!!

It's weird for me to think that Julie and my brother have been dating for almost six months now, but I try to separate her boyfriend Jake from the kid who used to try to pin me down and fart on my face just, oh, a year ago.

VIOLET GREENFIELD: the breakup plan isn't working?
DIANE SAWYER: well, sort of, but since i'm still in town we want to hang out
DIANE SAWYER: it's just hard
VIOLET GREENFIELD: tell me about it
DIANE SAWYER: trouble in paulo-land?

VIOLET GREENFIELD: not really
VIOLET GREENFIELD: everything's great here
DIANE SAWYER: but . . . ?
VIOLET GREENFIELD: i got this letter from roger

I wait for a full minute before getting impatient with Julie's silence. She's probably doing like ten things at once and can't pay attention to my IMs—annoying.

VIOLET GREENFIELD: hello?
DIANE SAWYER: what did it say?
VIOLET GREENFIELD: it was like this good-bye letter
VIOLET GREENFIELD: but then it said how he'd always be there for me no matter what
DIANE SAWYER: anything else?
VIOLET GREENFIELD: not really
VIOLET GREENFIELD: it was totally formal and serious
DIANE SAWYER: sounds like typical roger being dramatic
VIOLET GREENFIELD: yeah, I guess you're right
VIOLET GREENFIELD: it just seemed different somehow
VIOLET GREENFIELD: like it was really important to him to send it
DIANE SAWYER: he told me you had a fight the other day
VIOLET GREENFIELD: yeah, about paulo
VIOLET GREENFIELD: he's so overprotective of you and me that i'm sure he'd freak about any guys
DIANE SAWYER: yeah, he's just being himself
DIANE SAWYER: don't worry about it
DIANE SAWYER: you'll see him over fall break

After I log off with Julie, I feel kind of stupid for bringing up the letter with her. I mean, who cares if Roger wanted to be silly and send me a formal letter? That's all part of his quirky Roger-ness.

I push the thought out of my mind and tuck the letter into the small front pocket of my suitcase.

That night at dinner with Paulo, all confusion fades from my mind. Right in front of me, there's this amazingly talented, hot, kissable person. And he likes *me*. He tells me about how he knew he'd be a designer when he first sewed buttons on one of his father's creations at age five, how he dreams of showing a collection in Europe before he's twenty-five, how he used to think New York City was a whole country. I laugh at his stories and tell him about Julie and Roger, about how there's nothing like being at Carolina Beach with my feet in the sand, about how college basketball is like a religion in Chapel Hill. And as he laughs with me, I feel like I could talk to him forever.

"I have never met anyone like you, Violet," says Paulo as we walk back to the pool house. "I think I am falling in love."

I look at Paulo with what I hope is a pretty, intense, movie-style face like Scarlett used on Rhett when she got him to marry her. "Me too," I say.

That night we go further than I've ever even really imagined in bed. I mean, scary-but-awesome stuff involving tangled feet and lots of touching. But we don't have sex—and Paulo doesn't even ask me to. When I wake up and he's still next to me, I fight the urge to gasp audibly. *Please, please, please let me get what I want*, I sing to myself.

We spend the week shooting the Paulo Forte ads, which he's decided should be set in a studio after all, so that my "natural beauty" won't be in competition with any overly exotic surroundings. So basically, it's me and a purple velvet blanket, which is draped very strategically over my near-naked body. Paulo lets me wear these things called "breast petals" over my nipples, and I have these teensy panties on too. I may have come a long way with self-confidence, but I'm still not ready for my *Playboy* moment.

Everyone keeps throwing around words like *tasteful* and *classic* to make me feel better about this sexy shoot, but I'm actually much more comfortable than I thought I'd be. At first I worried that the purple blanket thing was going to be completely cheesy, but when I look at the outtakes, I can see how well the setup works. My best shots are both sexy and vulnerable. I look like a girl who's not completely sure of herself, but who is on the verge of realizing she has something special.

It feels like I've grown up five years during this time in Brazil with all that's happened, and I decide something really important: I want to lose my virginity to Paulo. Even though I feel adult and mature and sure of myself, I still have to check in with Julie before I do anything. I don't know at what age you stop running things by your best friend, but I know I'm not there yet.

VIOLET GREENFIELD: question
DIANE SAWYER: yes?
VIOLET GREENFIELD: what if I had sex with paulo?
DIANE SAWYER: OMG!!! what???!!
VIOLET GREENFIELD: would that make me a total slut?
DIANE SAWYER: no!! of course not!!
DIANE SAWYER: have you already??
VIOLET GREENFIELD: not yet! but i think I want to before i leave on Saturday. maybe tonight
DIANE SAWYER: so right before you come home, just to make it the most angsty experience possible?
VIOLET GREENFIELD: well yeah
DIANE SAWYER: i guess we're still two peas in a pod
VIOLET GREENFIELD: WHAT???
DIANE SAWYER: sorry to tell you that your little brother lost it before you
VIOLET GREENFIELD: wait—are you serious? whoa! when?
DIANE SAWYER: like two days ago

VIOLET GREENFIELD: and you're leaving for brown when?
DIANE SAWYER: wanted to tell you . . . we're going early so
    we can stop in DC and visit my dad's cousin
VIOLET GREENFIELD: early when?
DIANE SAWYER: tomorrow
VIOLET GREENFIELD: i won't see you!!
DIANE SAWYER: i know
DIANE SAWYER: but we'll talk every day

After Julie assures me some more that college will not mean the end of Violet-and-Julie, she wishes me good luck, gives me a "love you!" and logs off.

I'm not much into signs, but Julie and I did always say we'd do absolutely *everything* together. Somehow I always thought I'd want full details from her after she did the deed, but the fact that she did it with my little brother made me willing to skip the interrogation. Yuck. I shake off an involuntary shudder.

I dig through my luggage to find the lingerie from Dilecta, one of the designers in São Paulo Fashion Week. When I got this gift bag just three weeks ago, I actually laughed out loud at imagining myself wearing any of the items in it. But now, as I stare at the pink silk slip lined in hand-stitched lace, I think to myself, *Tonight's the night.*

Instead of letting Paulo come out to the pool house to meet me later, I decide to sneak into the main mansion early and surprise him. I'm wearing a Dilecta two-piece ensemble that is probably the tamest thing in the gift bag—it's like a silky pajama set. I'm being braver than I've ever been as far as sex is concerned, but I still can't rock the garter belt and fishnet stockings. Especially since I'm already wearing a cotton trench coat and heels to make myself a more grown-up seductress. I wonder what kinds of girls Paulo has dated in the past, but I'm trying to bar that thought from my mind—if I hear that he's dated some supermodel like Graciella, I'll chicken out.

As I sneak in through the back door by the kitchen, I see Elvis preparing a plate of cheese and grapes. There are two glasses of champagne set up on the tray. *Paulo must be planning another romantic night for us*, I think, feeling giddy.

I tiptoe up the stairs behind Elvis. I've never been to Paulo's room, so I follow carefully but quietly. Top of the stairs, third door on the right. Elvis knocks and enters, and I duck into the second door on the right, which I know is a way-fancy bathroom because I used it at the Fashion Week party. I look in the mirror and steel myself for this completely monumental thing I'm about to do. My hair is tousled in a deliberate bedhead way, and I just put on a little dab of blush and lipstick for a sexy flush. I think I'm ready. Right?

I hear Elvis head back down the stairs, and I step out into the hallway. Before I lose my nerve, I knock softly on Paulo's bedroom door.

My heart is pounding and my knees are shaking as Paulo says, "*Sim*, Elvis?"

I push open the door with a big smile on my face, partly because I want to look pretty and partly because I feel so dorky I can't help but grin at myself.

And that's when I see her. One of the too-skinny, attention-hogging models from the first night at dinner. Vidonia or Yelena or whatever. Smack-dab in the middle of a poufy red-and-gold, silk-sheeted, fit-for-a-king four-poster bed. With no clothes on.

As Paulo runs to the door to stop me from spinning on my heels and marching away, I slap him right across the face. Because no matter what his charming brain thinks of to say, there's really no way to explain a naked girl lying next to you in bed. That can mean only one thing.

I am so out of here.

eleven

I don't think anyone's ever packed as quickly as I did after seeing Paulo in bed with Skinnyskank, as I will now and forevermore refer to her. I deemed the situation emergency-credit-card-worthy, so I paid for my flight change with my parents' Visa. I got out of the mansion before Paulo could get dressed and come after me, so I'm not even sure if he tried. I was so angry that I told myself I didn't care either way. Now that I've been back in North Carolina for two weeks, though, the reality of the situation is starting to sting. Badly.

It's seven sixteen P.M. and I've been on the couch in the den, watching TV with the laptop by my side, for a good eight hours now. Neither Julie nor Roger has been online in *forever*—they're probably busy making new friends and binge drinking, or whatever you do at college orientation. Because I can't talk to them, I decide to finally set up my MySpace blog and record some grievances. Somehow it's more satisfying to air my feelings on the Web than it is to write them down in my old diary. I log on to myspace.com/violetgreenfield and let the blank box stare at me for ten minutes before I start.

> I feel like the older sister in *Dirty Dancing*. And not because my eyebrows are too thick. When you think you're in love with someone—when you *are* in love with someone—and they betray you, where do you turn? My solution so far today—day 13 since said betrayal occurred—has been a *Real World* marathon and two pints of ice cream (both Karamel Sutra, ironically). I'll probably never have sex. Ever. But worse, I'll probably never have someone to love who really loves me back.

I stop short of confessing to the virtual world that I pulled out my mom's eighties Whitney Houston CD and have been listening to "All at Once," this incredibly pathetic song about how Whitney was left for another woman, over and over again. "All at once, I'm drifting on a lonely sea, wishing you'd come back to me . . ." If I get into a song, I can listen to it on repeat *all day long*. Luckily, it's not available to add to my MySpace page, or else I'd probably really embarrass myself by setting it as my profile's theme.

My parents were really worried when I first got home, and not just because I charged $2,000 to their credit card (which I was promptly informed I'd be paying them back out of my modeling savings). I couldn't very well tell them the details of my devastation, but I managed to convey that I'd had a crush on a guy in Brazil and then I found out he had a girlfriend. Which in no way explains the severity of what I'm going through, but it seems about as much as my parents should know and they accepted it.

My aunt Rita called to tell me she'd heard about my heartache, and if I felt the need to get away from home, I was welcome at her house in Brooklyn anytime. Mom must have told her I'm averaging ten hours a day on the couch, a habit that I don't plan on changing until this pain in my chest subsides, but it was still nice of Rita to offer.

"Want some dinner, Vi?" Jake asks, mercifully interrupting my blogging as he lifts up my feet so he can join me on the couch. I nod and he hands me a bowl of heated-up SpaghettiO's, our favorite Mom-and-Dad-are-out meal. Jake is being really sweet . . . he probably understands my pain a little. I know he's going through his own stuff since he and Julie had to officially break up when she left for Brown. Chapel Hill seems dead without my two best friends here.

Jake and I veg out for another two hours while we watch *Groundhog Day* on TBS, and I think about how Roger proclaimed Bill Murray "the unrivaled king of comedy" when he talked his parents into renting the R-rated *Rushmore* in third grade. As the credits roll, I'm appreciating how my brother can just sit with me and not pry into why I'm too depressed to move when he suddenly looks at me and says, "So . . ."

I may have appreciated him too soon.

"So what?" I ask, staring at the TV to show him that I really don't want to engage in a meaningful brother-sister exchange right now.

"Well, I was thinking you should probably get off the couch tomorrow," he says.

"Thanks," I say, launching into my über-sarcastic tone. "And I should be taking advice from my sixteen-year-old jock brother why?"

"Whatever," he says, standing up and grabbing our now-crusty SpaghettiO bowls.

"Wait, Jake," I say, feeling guilty for being bratty to my little brother, who's only trying to be nice. "I'm sorry. I know you miss Julie too."

He stares at the carpet for a minute, and I realize that I've never seen him this vulnerable. My little brother, who's always been a star athlete and Dad's favorite, is heartsick.

"I do miss Julie," he admits. Then he looks up at me. "But I miss you too."

I raise my eyebrows. "Me?" I ask.

"Yeah, you!" he says, kicking my shin. "You left all of a sudden last year and then this summer you, like, went away to another country.

And now you're here, but you're moping around like you're seriously depressed. And soon you'll be in college and gone for good."

"Well, you will too in like two years," I say.

"I know," he says. "I guess things just changed faster than I thought they would. One day it was the four of us, and now it's just me at dinner with Mom and Dad."

"You were always the dinner star," I say. "I just filled in some conversation when basketball season was over."

"It's not the same without you," he says, looking so sincere that I'm about to reach out and hug him.

And just when I think we're going to have this big Hallmark moment, Jake leans in and burps right in my face. One of those big burps that comes with a gush of smelly air.

"Sick!" I shout, while Jake doubles over in laughter. Then he stands up and brings our dishes into the kitchen.

Behind his back, I smile. I had no idea he missed me.

I open my laptop again, wondering if anyone interesting is online. As I click back to my profile, I notice that there are some new friend requests. Uh, 376 to be exact—*what?* I scroll through the unfamiliar faces of girls my age—and more than a few guys. Last year when I got some notoriety from modeling, I had a few dozen friend adds, but nothing like this.

"Jake!" I yell.

"What?" he pops his head into the den.

"I have like four hundred friend adds on MySpace," I say.

"Probably because of the *Teen Fashionista* story," he replies nonchalantly.

"It's *out?!*" I yell. "Why haven't I seen it?"

"It's right on the coffee table, dumbass," says Jake. "Mom left it for you there yesterday. Maybe if you got out of your own mopey MySpace-and-crappy-movies mode for a minute, you'd notice it."

I roll my eyes at Jake and reach for the magazine, which—true—is sitting on the center of the coffee table. The profile is pretty small, just a "rising star" kind of article, and Chloe didn't do a bad job. There are quotes from Julie—as well as a tiny picture of us in the corner. It's the last line of the story, though, that makes me catch my breath.

"So why should the world take notice of Violet Greenfield? Well, just ask her friend Roger: 'Anyone who meets Violet for five minutes will fall in love with her. I did.'"

The next day, I convince my parents that I should take Rita up on her offer for me to visit New York. The reasons I give them are (1) I need a change of scenery to get over my crush, and (2) Angela wants to prep me for European shows, which, after all, are the reason I deferred college.

Both reasons are true, but here is my own motivation for flying up to the city: (1) With the explosion of my MySpace page, thanks to the *Teen Fashionista* article, I feel this new energy, like I have fans or something. I am totally ready to get back into the modeling world. (2) Fuck Paulo. (3) I've *got* to talk to Roger.

When I call Angela to tell her I'll be up in New York, she's thrilled. Apparently, the ad I shot for Paulo Forte is going up as a big billboard in São Paulo next week, and there's good news from Paris too.

"The photos were stunning, Violet, really," she coos. Obviously she didn't hear a thing about my soured romance, not that she would care. "This billboard will be a great addition to your portfolio, and Paris is already asking about you." She explains that there's an emerging Parisian designer named Christian Blanc who saw some of my runway shots from Brazil and has chosen an image of me for a project he's working on with Lancôme. He's designing new Juicy Tubes that will include one of his sketches on the packaging—a sketch of *me*! Angela says they want the new line of glosses to appeal to jet-setting fashion icons, and Christian thinks I'm perfect. *Can you imagine?*

I get to talk to him on the phone the next day as he's sketching, and he's incredibly cool. He's really young—like in his twenties—and he just seems like he wants to talk about who I am and what I like to do. Christian even tells me that he puts out bread for models at castings, which is so not something I've ever seen—but I love it! We talk for about half an hour, and then he says he's got an idea of who I am, so we say good-bye. When Angela e-mails me a jpeg of the sketch later in the week, I'm beyond excited. The drawing is both cute and sophisticated, according to my dad.

"Next up will be the Violet Barbie doll," says Jake, rolling his eyes, but he gives me a hug and I know he thinks it's cool that all the girls at Chapel Hill High School will be carrying around an image of me when these Juicy Tubes come out.

I start to think of the work I did with Paulo as a big stepping stone, which helps me frame it more like I used him than he used me. And although not so deep down I'm still incredibly hurt, I resolve not to let that stop me as I head into this next phase of my career: The European Shows.

I get to the city a few days later, and I IM Roger to say I'm in town for work. I try to sound super casual, and we agree to meet at Two Boots, a tiny pizza place near his dorm at NYU. When I walk in, he isn't there yet, so I grab a sausage-and-onion slice and sit down to wait. I realize I'm kind of nervous to see Roger, which is so weird. But ever since I saw the closing line of the *Teen Fashionista* story, I've been wondering what he meant by "in love." Like, did he mean . . . with me? For real?

When I see him walk in, my heart pounds a little harder. Roger's wearing a plain white T-shirt with a navy blue hoodie. He has on dark jeans with a pair of brown-and-orange sneakers, and his hair is longer than it was in July—with a bit more pomade, I notice. His signature black-frame glasses turn sideways when he cocks his head and gives me a smile. He looks really good.

"Hey," I say, pulling him into the booth for a hug. He squeezes tightly before breaking away and hopping up to grab two slices of pepperoni. When he sits back down again, the first thing he says is, "You look great!"

"Really?" I laugh. "I've been on a steady diet of ice cream and cheeseburgers for two weeks."

"Seriously, Violet, you were starting to look frail after last year's modeling stuff," he says, biting into his first slice. "Now you're like a thin girl, but not skin and bones. Maybe Brazil was good for you."

I look down at my plate and my eyes start to fill with tears as I think about Paulo.

"I didn't mean . . ." starts Roger. "I'm sorry if I . . ."

"No, it's okay," I say, swallowing my sadness. So much for my resolve not to show the hurt. Somehow Roger always brings out my true emotions.

"From the little that Julie's told me, that Paulo guy sounds like a Class-A tosser," says Roger. "I mean, the guy's name sounds all exotic, but it's just fancy for *Paul Strong*, right? Loser."

"I know," I say, lifting my head and banishing images of Skinnyskank from my mind. "But I don't want to talk about that." Even Roger's jokes can't cheer me up right now.

"Okay," says Roger. "Me neither. Let's talk about how cool it is that we're both in New York living semiadult lives now."

"I've been a semiadult for a while," I say, smiling.

"Well, excuse me, Miss Maturity," says Roger. "I guess I'm just catching up to you. But seriously, I love NYU. I have this amazing freshman comp class—the teacher is so smart that I think she might know more than I do."

"Shock," I say dryly, but I can't stop the excited ramble that's coming out of Roger's mouth.

"My history class actually seems worthwhile too, and my roommate isn't the brightest bulb, but he did show me how to—"

"Roger," I interrupt, afraid I'll lose my nerve if I don't bring up the *Teen Fashionista* thing, like, now.

"Huh?" he says, digging into his slice during this small break in chatter.

"Did you see our *Teen Fashionista* story?" I ask.

"You mean your *Teen Fashionista* story?" he says. "Of course! Chloe got me an early copy. She's the best, Violet—I know she's like twenty-two, but I really think older women suit me—"

"What?" I say, quietly, almost to myself. And Roger must not hear me because he keeps talking about Chloe and how she's been showing him around the city and introducing him to her magazine friends and taking him to media parties, which is so Roger's dream world.

When he finally stops, I've run through a gamut of emotions. I came here thinking that Roger maybe said that he loved me in a national magazine—that he was trying to tell me something he'd kept secret—but it turns out he was just being quotable for his new *girl-friend*. I think back to when Chloe programmed Roger's phone number into her cell and how it made me cringe even then. But why should I care? Roger's just a friend.

"That's great!" I say.

Roger looks at me funny. "You knew about Chloe, right?" he says. "I assumed Julie told you."

"Oh, yeah, well, actually . . ." I stutter. "I didn't. I mean, you and Julie have been really busy with all this college stuff, and I've been kind of hibernating at home, so . . ."

Roger's still looking at me with a weird expression on his face.

"But it doesn't matter!" I say, a little too perkily. "I know now! And I'm *so* happy for you!"

"Cool," he says, reaching over to grab my crust, which I won't eat since I hate dense bread. I love that he knows me that well.

"So this is your town now," I say, trying to move the topic of conversation along as I realize there's no way I'm going to ask Roger what he meant by the letter he sent to me in São Paulo and his quote in *Teen Fashionista*. It's obvious that I'm completely reading into things because I'm in a heartbreak fog over Paulo.

"Well, I don't know if it's my town *yet*," says Roger, standing up and offering me a hand out of the booth. "But Chloe wants to go out with us when she gets done with work tonight, so we'll definitely do something cool."

After *work*. Roger is dating someone who actually has a job. Like a parent-style job.

"Oh," I say, forcing a smile. "That sounds fun."

twelve

After an almost unbearable night with the entity known as RoChlo where she blew in his ear a total of four times—and he actually seemed to *like* it—I'm finally back in Brooklyn, furiously dialing Julie's cell.

Thank God she picks up.

"Jules!"

"Violet!"

"It's so good to hear your voice!" I shout.

"Are you being passive-aggressive?" she asks. "Because I'm so sorry I haven't been around lately. It's just that everything at Brown is—"

And I really don't think I can stand to listen to another "college is so great" rant, so I interrupt.

"Forget it—I'm fine," I say. I really wasn't being passive-aggressive, but I do want to get to the point. "Jules, what is the deal with Chloe?" I ask, in a semiaccusing tone.

"You're in New York already?" she says, guiltily.

"Oh yeah," I say. "And I just spent four hours with the new Mr. and Mrs."

"Painful?" Julie asks.

"Excruciating," I reply. And then I tell Julie about how Roger's *Teen Fashionista* quote really confused me. But she blows it off by saying how she herself could have said the exact same thing, and how it was definitely just a "Violet's my best friend" kind of quote, not a confession of romantic love.

"Great," I say. "Now I feel even more stupid for bringing it up."

"Don't," says Julie. "You're probably just projecting old emotions for Paulo onto the closest guy around."

"What does that mean, oh life-coached one?" I ask.

"Just that you're kind of confused right now," says Julie. "You recently had your boyfriend or whatever cheat on you, which sucks, and you probably wanted to run to Roger and get all the affection that he usually showers on you. You've never had to share him before. You're jealous."

"I am not!" I protest.

"Really, Violet?" Julie asks. "Because it sounds like you're pretty upset over this Chloe thing."

"Only because she's super annoying!" I say.

"Okay," says Julie, sounding like she doesn't believe me.

When we hang up, I'm more confused than ever. I turn on my computer and pray that one of Rita's neighbors is more technologically advanced than she is. Score—there are ten wireless networks in the area. I find one without password protection and log on to myspace.com/violetgreenfield.

When you have a best friend for like 95% of your life, you expect certain things. You expect him to be completely honest with you, you expect to know what he means when he says he loves you, you expect him to clue in when you're feeling heartsick and vulnerable. And you expect him to not like it when someone blows in his ear, which is something we always thought was completely gross. You expect him not to change.

I hit Post and shut my laptop before I can decide not to leave my blog entry up. I know Roger will see it, but maybe he should. Maybe I want him to. Maybe he ought to know that I'm confused—and that I need him to be there for *me*. Not that cloying Chloe.

The next day I meet Angela at Henri Bendel, the store where I was first outfitted for my Fashion Week go-sees about a year ago. When I walk in, I immediately spot Ginny Hart, the girl who did my personal shopping last time.

"Hi there," I say, popping up behind her.

"Oh . . ." she says, looking slightly worried as her eyes trail over me. "Violet, hi. Is, um, Angela here?"

"I don't know," I say. "She just said to meet her at two P.M."

"Oh, okay," says Ginny, starting to stride toward the elevator. "Why don't you go on upstairs and I'll wait for Angela?" She inserts her VIP key and pushes the button for the private floor, the one with plush carpets and gold mirrors that's reserved for actresses and models and other big spenders.

When the doors open, I see a familiar face. Veronica is slouched on an oversized chair in the corner of the room. She looks bored with her legs tossed over an arm of the chair as she waits, I presume, for Angela.

"Hey," says Veronica, in a quiet tone that sounds almost . . . insecure.

"Hey," I reply, not really sure what to say, and surprised to see her.

"I heard what happened with Paulo," says Veronica. The girl doesn't do small talk.

"Look, if you're going to launch into an I-told-you-so speech, I'm really not in the mood," I say.

"I wasn't going to, Violet," she says, sighing. "I'm really sorry things worked out that way."

"Yeah, well, it doesn't matter," I say, softening a little. "You were right and I was naïve and I should have listened to you."

"No," says Veronica. "I should let you be you. You go with your heart on things, V. There's nothing wrong with that. I'm just so jaded that I think everyone else should be too for some reason. Besides, I was totally out of line."

"You mean with that 'still a virgin' comment?" I ask, trying to sound mean but failing. The truth is, I feel too tired to stay mad at Veronica; besides, I could use a friend right now.

She winces. "Yeah, uh, sorry about that," she says. "I'm so used to getting in the bitchy last line that it's kind of automatic."

"It's okay," I say. "And it's still true."

"Well that's good news, Greenfield," says Veronica, laughing. "You don't want to lose your innocence with a—what would Roger call him?—a douchebag?"

"Yeah," I say. "But he called Paulo a 'tosser' last night. I think he has new college insults now."

Veronica smiles. "How is jolly old Roger?" she asks.

"Oh, fine," I say, frowning. "He's dating some *Teen Fashionista* assistant who likes to blow in his ears."

"Ew," says Veronica. "How old is she?"

"Twenty-two," I say.

"What kind of a self-respecting twenty-two-year-old dates an NYU freshman?" asks Veronica, scowling.

"Well, Roger's really mature," I say. "And he looks like he could be twenty-two. It's weird—it's like he's lived in New York forever and he's only been here for a few weeks."

"Hipster types are like that," says Veronica. "So are you really over the Paulo thing?"

"Yeah," I say unconvincingly. But the truth is—I'm not. I still fall asleep listening to my iPod set to a playlist that's called "São Paulo" but it might as well be called just "Paulo." It has all the songs I listened to at the pool house every night, and a couple that we heard on the super-romantic dates on yachts and out on the town and at the beach under the stars. It almost seems like I dreamed it all.

But my official line is: I'm over it.

"Did it take a couple weeks of couch time with Ben and Jerry, though?" asks Veronica.

"Yeah," I say. "Am I that generic? How could you tell?"

"No reason," she says. "You just look like you haven't exactly been pumping iron lately."

I look down at my stomach, feeling suddenly self-conscious.

"Violet, I did not mean that to be mean at all," says Veronica, sensing my discomfort as she stands up and walks over to me. "Seriously. I just noticed that—"

Ding. The elevator bell rings and I can hear Angela's voice before the door even opens.

"Violet, let me see you," she's yelling. "Come here!"

I start toward Angela and I can already see a shadow of horror on her face.

"Oh no, no, no, no, no!" she gasps. "You must have put on five pounds since I saw you in Brazil! Don't tell me you're one of those girls who eats *more* when she's depressed. Darling, I was expecting you to be even *thinner* after your little destroyed dalliance with that playboy Paulo!"

"I told you, Angela," says Ginny, sighing. "She looks like a four. Possibly even a six."

"This is not good, Violet," says Angela, staring at me very sternly. "You must lose weight. Immediately. Do whatever it takes. Veronica, why don't you show Violet that cleanse diet thing that you did last year?"

"You mean the cleanse I did last year just before I was hospitalized for an eating disorder and drug addiction?" asks Veronica sarcastically.

"Exhaustion, dear," says Angela hurriedly, motioning to Ginny like she doesn't want Ginny to know the details of Veronica's stay upstate. "You were hospitalized for exhaustion. And the cleanse had nothing to do with it." It's amazing that Angela's still smiling through tight lips.

While the three of them chatter around me, I start to feel incredibly uncomfortable. They're discussing *my* body, *my* waistline, *my* thighs. But no one's actually talking to *me*.

"Give her everything in a two," Angela says to Ginny as they go through racks and pick out the clothes that I'll wear when we travel to Europe next week to meet with designers. "You'll lose the weight this week, Violet," says Angela, turning to me. "Or else you'll only book those BMI-happy Madrid shows. Good thing we're going to Spain first!" And with that, she exits, leaving me more insecure than I've felt in months.

When I get back to Brooklyn, I go online and immediately research crash diets. I know that Julie and Roger would die if they heard about me doing this—especially as I find ridiculous references to the cabbage soup diet and the all-grapefruit plan. I think of last year when I moved into the model apartment and Sam told me that almost everyone gets an eating disorder eventually. I wonder if grapefruits for five days counts as a disorder.

In between Googling my perfect diet, I log on to myspace .com/violetgreenfield. There are a few responses to my post about Roger, though none from the man himself. I click on his profile and see that he hasn't logged on in six days. Must be too busy getting his earwax blown out. The responses to my whining, though, are really sweet and supportive—most from girls I don't even know personally. They're so nice, in fact, that I decide to blog about my current dilemma.

Five pounds. That's it. Just five. How can five pounds send everyone into such a tizzy? So I got my heart smashed into tiny little pieces and wanted to relax for a few days and drown my sorrows in the delicious vanilla-and-candy flavors of Karamel Sutra. Does that mean I should be in danger of losing my career? No. But I am. Or at least it feels that way.

I post the entry and decide to stop Googling for eating disorders. I call Veronica and arrange to meet her at a coffee shop in Brooklyn.

"Want me to come to Park Slope?" asks Veronica.

"That's okay," I say. "I can meet you in Carroll Gardens." The neighborhood where Veronica has her studio apartment is a long—but totally doable—walk from Aunt Rita's neighborhood. I need to burn off the fiber cereal I ate this morning anyway.

By the time I get to Court Street, I'm exhausted. I flop down onto a couch across from Veronica, who's got a pot of tea in front of her.

"Green chai?" she asks. "You look like you could use some antioxidants."

"Is it—?" I start.

"Fattening? Caloric? Thunder-thigh enhancing?" she says, frowning. "No, Violet. It's not."

"I'm sorry," I say, feeling lame. "It's just that—"

"You don't have to explain to *me*, sweetie," interrupts Veronica. "I've been there and then some. But seriously, please don't start researching the cabbage soup diet so you can lose the weight by next week."

The guilt must show on my face, because then Veronica says, "You already did that, didn't you?"

I nod guiltily.

"Well it totally doesn't work," says Veronica. "Trust me."

Then my cell phone beeps and I pull up a text message from Angela: "Vito's salon at noon tomorrow," I read aloud.

"She's going to make you get the thin haircut," says Veronica.

"The what?" I ask.

"The thin haircut—the one where Vito throws shadows over your face with your hair to make you look more gaunt," she explains. "Angela made me do it once before, but if you ask me it's just a marketing technique by Vito—it doesn't really work."

"Am I that fat?" I ask, looking down at my tea and wondering if I should even risk the fifteen calories that are lurking in its clear green waters.

"Violet, listen," says Veronica. "You know you're not. I know you're not. Hell, even Angela knows you're not. Really. But she's thinking about the people who are going to pinch your hips in Paris, the designers who will judge you by the shadow of your collarbone in Milan."

"But I thought everyone was moving toward a healthier look," I say. Despite the fact that I don't read the paper much, I've finally picked up on everyone in the industry talking about the body mass index requirements.

"Oh, they are," says Veronica. "At least in the public relations sense. But it'll take a while before they can wean themselves off of the look they've loved since heroine chic took hold. And Angela knows that."

"So what can I do?" I ask.

"Get the haircut to please her," says Veronica. "As for dieting, just cut out some calories each day. Even if you've only lost three pounds by next week, it'll show Angela you're trying."

"Okay," I say, glad that Veronica and I made up. What would I do without her advice?

For dinner that night, Rita suggests Chinese. As she dials Uncle Leo's, I request steamed vegetables—no rice.

"Not the usual?" she asks, as she dials.

The usual is sesame chicken. I'm pretty sure that fried and honey-glazed bird is a no-no for me this week.

"Nah," I say nonchalantly. At least I hope it sounds nonchalant.

"Just vegetables?" she asks, raising an eyebrow at me.

"Yeah," I say.

"No chicken? No beef?" she asks. Man, she is persistent.

"Just the vegetables," I say, turning my attention to the deodorant ad on television and staring really hard, like I'm fascinated by the new sweat-fighting technology advances.

When the food arrives, the peas and carrots and mushrooms look pretty limp. I've never ordered from the "healthy choices" section of Uncle Leo's menu before, and as I take a bite, I vow never to do it again. Everything is bland and soggy—even the snap peas.

"Enjoying your rabbit food?" asks Rita as she digs into her delicious-looking lo mein noodles.

This losing five pounds thing is going to be tough.

thirteen

A week later, I'm on an Iberia flight from JFK to Madrid. I'm trying hard not to let Angela's weight comments get to me, but I have definitely cut back on my portions to the point where I always feel a little pang of hunger. I talked to Veronica and she said that sensation is pretty standard, and that I'll get used to it during the shows. "You can always start eating more again after the Fashion Weeks if you need to," she said. I wish she were coming to Spain, but she's staying in New York to do some editorial shoots.

Because Angela is traveling with me, we're flying business class, which is completely thrilling. There's free champagne and strawberries when we board, and after takeoff I notice that there's a menu in my seat offering a choice of amazing-sounding three-course meals.

"What are you going to get?" I ask Angela, who I can tell is annoyed by my excitement and being generally no fun.

"I'm going to get a Perrier and an Ambien," she says. "And so will you if you want to keep that stomach flat." With that, she pulls on her sleeping mask and reclines to a practically horizontal position.

I decide to order what I want and just take a bite of each dish. I haven't been able to diet too much—after the first night of soggy vegetables I realized that the sacrifice of taste is just too great. But I did lose two pounds anyway, probably from just cutting out the pint-a-day ice cream habit I had going.

I also went to Vito's salon and got a really cute haircut. I don't know if it makes me look "gaunt" as Veronica suggested, but it's an angular bob that frames my face really nicely, and he added some blond highlights so my hair has a coppery shimmer. The cut makes me feel more mature somehow. I've been swinging my hair around and making pouty-lip faces to myself as I whisper, "I'm so over Paulo" in the mirror. Julie told me to do that (no doubt on the advice of her life coach) and it never ceases to make me feel better, if only because I end up laughing at how ridiculous I'm being.

I take small bites of the airplane food—which is actually one of my favorite things to eat, even in coach, I'm learning—and leave most of the meal on my plate. Then I put on my eye mask and recline my seat a bit, but not as much as Angela's, because if we were at the same angle it might feel like we're in bed together. And that is not something I want to experience.

In Madrid, we check into a hotel in an area called Sol. It's like the Times Square of Spain, our taxi driver tells us. There are definitely major neon lights in the center of Sol, but the buildings are very low—like maybe five or six stories—and they're completely enchanting, more like stone mansion blocks from another century than the cold, reflective skyscrapers of New York.

"*Que bonito*," I say, as the driver nods in satisfaction—he seems proud of his city. My high school Spanish isn't getting me very far, but it's better than Angela's way of speaking to people here, which is in loud, slow English. I can't wait to get away from her.

"You've got the whole day, Vicarious Violet," says Angela, handing me my key card. "I'll see you tomorrow morning in the lobby for some appointments, but in the meantime, *experiencia la España!*" She says those last words as if she's some dramatic flamenco performer, and I grab my key and rush to distance myself from her as the bellhop winces.

I drop off my suitcase in a small but elegant room with lace curtains and a royal-blue carpet. It's less boutique-chic than the São Paulo hotel, but this one has some old-world charm, as my father would say. Just picturing the room in Brazil makes me think of Paulo and the night he met me at midnight and took me to the ice runway. I grab my iPod with a sigh and decide to do some major wallowing—disguised as exploration, of course.

The concierge tells me that Madrid's big park—El Retiro—is a nice walk away, so I head in the direction he points toward and set my iPod to the "São Paulo" playlist. I'm a masochist of the first degree, I acknowledge, as I wander past historic stone buildings and snap a camera-phone photo of *Museos de Jamon*—which I'm guessing are butcher shops, but it's funny that they translate to "Ham Museum."

When I get to the park, I'm in a completely bittersweet zone, a montage of Paulo memories running through my head, set to the Shins' "Kissing the Lipless." But at the same time, I'm in *Madrid*, seeing street performers who paint themselves completely gray to look like statues, venders selling churros (which seem to be sticks of fried dough dipped in sugar), and an open-air café where gorgeous dark-haired women and suavely dressed men smoke cigarettes and listen to the live music that drifts over the grassy hill. It's beautiful.

Back at the hotel, I feel a little better. I start unpacking—dresses hung, boots stacked and stuffed with shoehorns, blouses in drycleaning bags to be pressed by the hotel. Angela taught me well. As I reach the bottom of the suitcase, I notice an envelope—Roger's letter. I was in such a lovesick daze when I got home from Brazil that I never threw it out. I read over it quickly—*I will always be within shouting distance, always ready to rush to your aid, always there in case you need me. Always, Your Roger.* Yeah right. He was so busy with Chloe in New York that he didn't even have time to see me again before I flew to Spain. I consider ripping up the letter and throwing it in the garbage, but then I decide it could be a good guilt-inducing tool for Roger one day.

The concierge told me that Sol is Madrid's nightlife neighborhood, but I'm not feeling much like a party. I settle in with a jar of olives from the minibar and a can of regular—not diet—Coke. I deserve some sugar.

I pull out my laptop and log on to myspace.com/violetgreenfield. There are lots of comments on my post about dieting from last week, I notice. Some are girls telling me to think healthy—to eat right and exercise. Others are bizarre suggestions of how to lose ten pounds in a week, including harebrained ideas about subsisting on water and saltines. A few even reference *ana*, which I know is code for anorexia. It's kind of scary. I post a response to clarify that I'm really not a full-on eating disorder case:

Hey thanks for all the support out there. I'm definitely doing better—two pounds lighter and in Madrid now for fashion show castings! I am so lame I couldn't do any diets that required self-control but I am trying to eat smaller meals (like tonight I'm having olives and a Coke in my hotel room—haha). Anyway, thanks again!!

Hopefully that will clarify that I'm just a regular girl trying to lose extra pounds—not a head-case model with eating issues. I was going to blog about how much I'm missing Paulo, but I decide that's stupid. Besides, what if he sees it? Do they use MySpace in Brazil?

I turn on the TV and watch *Rear Window*—a Hitchcock movie I've seen a hundred times—in Spanish. I can almost follow it for a while, but then the effort must be too much because I fall fast asleep by nine P.M.

The next morning, Angela is teeming with energy at eight A.M. Which, I will point out, is like two A.M. New York time. I went to bed early but I woke up about four times in the middle of the night.

I pull on a pair of jeans and a loose, deconstructed blouse that hides the slight stomach bulge sticking out over my size 2s. I still don't know why Angela wouldn't let me get anything in a 4. Is it that big a deal? I run a brush through my hair, dab lip stain on both my cheeks and lips, and rush down to the lobby.

"Oh, honey," says Angela as she greets me with a skim latte. "Jet lag is a bitch." Then she hands me my schedule, complete with eleven castings. Ouch.

The day is a whirlwind of meetings that go like this: "Hi, I'm Violet Greenfield." I hand the designers my book, they page through, and then they tell me to walk. I walk. They smile. I move along to the next cattle call.

When I meet Angela for dinner at the hotel, I warn her that I might fall asleep in my gazpacho.

"Oh, don't be dramatic, Vulnerable Violet," she coos. "You did well today—I've already gotten three calls to book you."

"Really?" I ask, perking up. "Does that mean I can stop fasting and order an actual meal with this bowl of tomato juice?"

"Hold on, Piggly Wiggly," says Angela. "Madrid has those new rules about BMI, so they're looking to book some heavier girls. Not so in Paris."

"Are you saying that I'm one of the heavier girls?" I ask, bewildered.

"Well," says Angela, leaning in. "You're not the skinniest anymore, darling. Runway is real life—there's no retouching. They want you perfect."

For the rest of the meal I push my spoon around the bowl and plaster a fake smile on my face as Angela rattles on about some old boyfriend she'd like to catch up with in Milan. *I can't believe that I'm one of the fat ones.* I glance down at my stomach a few times—it is rolling over the top of my jeans a little bit, but isn't that normal?

I excuse myself before the check comes and head up to my room. One thing Angela said keeps ringing in my ears: "They want you perfect." I need a plan of attack for dealing with this bulk. And fast.

fourteen

I attempt a run in the park at seven A.M., before I have to meet Angela, but it's miserable. I nearly faint after ten minutes, and I learn that I should definitely eat something before trying to jog.

At breakfast, Angela tells me I've booked eight shows.

"You're definitely making a name for yourself here, Violet," she says, smiling. "But remember, you can't gain weight like Tyra, darling, and still expect to book jobs." Seeing the look on my face, she backpedals a bit. "You're not Tyra. Yet."

I'm starting to get angry about all this fat talk. I spent like half an hour in front of the mirror last night, pinching my waist and looking at myself from all angles. It made me feel awkward and awful. But I don't know how to tell Angela that I'm upset. She'll just think I can't handle the pressure. So I stay silent.

Still, because Angela's happy with my bookings, and shows don't start until later in the week, she gives me some time to myself. "Go find a Spanish fling," she says, laughing. "You're good with foreign men."

I think she meant that in a nice way, but it's hard to tell with Angela. I have too much on my mind to try to be social anyway, though I did get some invitations to pre–Fashion Week parties. I text Sam and find out that she's going to be in Milan and Paris coming up, so at least I'll have some friends around if I make it that far.

I check my e-mail and see that there's a message from Jake, which is weird because my brother has, like, never e-mailed me. The subject is "URGENT."

"v, call my cell. j"

I decide to call him from the hotel phone and let Angela pick up the charges.

As the phone rings, I glance at the clock. It's noon here, so it's . . . oops! Six A.M. in North Carolina. I'm about to hang up when I hear a groggy, "Hello?"

"Jake, hey," I say. "I'm so sorry I—"

"Violet!" Jake shout-whispers, suddenly sounding super awake. "I wasn't sure you knew, but I wanted to call you because I know how when you're traveling you can get kind of spacey and . . ."

I let him ramble on, but he's being vague and I'm still confused, so I interrupt. "Jake, what's going on?"

"Well, it'll probably blow over soon, but it seemed like you should—"

"Jake!" I shout, now starting to get a little worried. "What *is* it?"

"Can you get online?" he asks. "Go to nypost.com and click on Page Six gossip."

I open my laptop and go to the newspaper site. When I click on Page Six, I see a photo of myself that must be from last spring. The headline reads, "Stick Model Talking: 'Five Pounds May Cost Me My Career.'"

"But what?" I stutter. "I didn't say that—"

"They took quotes from MySpace," says Jake. "Violet, you should not be publicly posting your blog."

"Have you been reading my entries?" I ask.

"What little brother wouldn't peek at his sister's diary?" He laughs. "But my snooping is the least of your problems."

I'm furiously scanning the rest of the item. There's a line from the post that I just put up two days ago about eating olives and Coke for dinner—but it's completely out of context and makes it seem like I'm some crazed anorexic girl. "Are they allowed to do this?" I whisper, almost to myself.

"Your profile is public, Violet," says Jake, sighing. "Didn't you pay attention during all those Internet safety lessons Mom and Dad made us sit through at dinner?"

I log on to myspace.com/violetgreenfield and immediately change my settings to private, so that only people I'm friends with can see what I write. I notice I have a lot of new messages—a few from Roger and Julie.

"Jake," I say, "I have to go. Thanks for telling me, though."

"Okay," he says, and I can hear the worry in his voice. "Be careful, Vi."

"I will," I say. "You don't think Mom and Dad will see this—do you?"

"Not unless education blogs pick it up," says Jake. "And I'll prescan the newspaper for the next few days, just in case."

"Thanks, Jake," I say. "Really."

When we hang up, I start reading through my MySpace messages. Roger saw the quotes in a super snarky write-up on gawker .com. I realize that I have a bunch of messages from adults—like reporters from newspapers around the country who want to talk to me about my blog.

Brrring, brrring. The phone double-rings and I jump a little, startled.

"Hello?" I say, half expecting it to be Roger for some reason.

But it's Angela. And she is livid. She uses more obscenities than I ever thought could fit in one sentence as she orders me to delete my blog immediately and tells me she can't deal with me right now while she's busy meeting with Spanish designers. "I'm trying to build a career for you, and you are fucking self-sabotaging!" she screams. Then she hangs up.

That went better than I thought it would.

I know I should listen to Angela and delete my MySpace profile, but I don't want to lose all the "friends" I have. They really feel like fans at this point—like girls who are reading it because they admire something about me. My hand is hovering over the Delete Profile button when I see that Roger is logging on to IM.

VIOLET GREENFIELD: up so early?

RC1: 8 am class, señorita.

VIOLET GREENFIELD: so you saw the post

RC1: I saw Gawker, and, yeah, I kinda figured the story would catch on.

VIOLET GREENFIELD: but why were media people looking at a teenager's myspace page anyway?

RC1: They weren't on a teenager's MySpace, they were on an international runway model's MySpace. I'm sure they troll that shit all the time to find filler to write about.

VIOLET GREENFIELD: and the *post?*

RC1: There's been all that news about how models are too thin—it's a natural fit. I wouldn't be surprised if the *Times* picked up something about you.

VIOLET GREENFIELD: i think they sent me a message on my-space

RC1: Really? That's awesome!

VIOLET GREENFIELD: what are you talking about? this could ruin my career!

RC1: Or make it.

VIOLET GREENFIELD: huh?

RC1: Think about it, Violet. You could talk about the pressures and how you had a momentary lapse where you tried to lose weight even though you're, like, the skinniest girl on the planet.

RC1: It was a momentary lapse, right?

VIOLET GREENFIELD: i guess

RC1: Not convincing, but I know you'll come to your senses. Especially your sense of wanting to eat pizza freely.

RC1: But no crusts. ☺

I laugh.

VIOLET GREENFIELD: whoa—an emoticon from mr. anti-smiley?!

RC1: I have to run to class. Think about it though, Vi.

RC1 has signed off.

Smooth of Roger not to mention the blog post that I put up about *him*, but I'm still glad we talked.

Before I lose my nerve, I decide to respond to some of the reporters requesting interviews. Maybe Roger's right. Maybe this is my chance to do something good within the modeling world, my chance to make a difference for some of those girls who made "ana" comments on my blog.

I MySpace-message a few reporters, giving them the name of my hotel and the main number. It couldn't hurt to do an interview or two, and maybe I can defend myself a little, lest readers of Gawker.com and the *Post* think I'm a dumb, skinny asshole.

The first phone call comes about two minutes after I send the messages.

"Hi, this is Kevin O'Brien from the *Chicago Tribune*," says the very businesslike voice.

"Hi," I say. "This is Violet Greenfield."

"Violet, we're on the record here. Can you tell me what you think of the modeling industry's stick-thin beauty standard?" asks Kevin, in a rapid-fire voice.

"Uh . . ." I stutter. *This guy does not beat around the bush.* "I think it's hard for models to ever feel they're thin enough."

"Right, right, and like you said on your blog, if you gain five pounds you're in danger of losing work?" asks Kevin.

"Definitely," I say, realizing I have some things to get off my chest here. "I mean, what girl at this age isn't going through some changes with her body? Isn't it kind of cruel to make a big deal over fluctuations of a few pounds? Why make normal girls—who would never consider going on weird restrictive diets—feel like they have to be skin and bones?"

I can hear Kevin typing away, and I know I'm giving him good quotes.

"And these are girls who are your age? Eighteen?" he asks.

"Yes, and some even younger," I say, on a roll. "Imagine being thirteen or fourteen and told that you have to conform to this impossible standard when you're still growing."

"I can't imagine," says Kevin. I can tell he's on my side. "So how do you handle the pressures personally?"

"Well, I admit that I've been hard on myself," I say, wondering where my poise and eloquence is coming from. I'm actually good at this. "I can't think of a single model who hasn't tried to limit her portions or crash-diet at some point."

"Are you saying that you're done being hard on yourself? That you're embracing a new aesthetic as one of the promising up-and-comers in the modeling world?"

I pause for a moment, considering the questions. "Yes," I say. "That's what I'm saying. I'm saying I have a few pounds more on my frame this year—and I booked eight shows in Madrid anyway."

"Is the consciousness changing, Violet?" asks Kevin. "On the part of the models, I mean."

"I don't know," I say honestly. "But *my* consciousness is changing."

Kevin thanks me and hangs up. I don't even have time to think about what I just said before the phone rings again—a reporter in Boston. Before the day is out, I've answered the same kinds of questions for about ten different newspapers.

Later in the afternoon, I ask the front desk to send any calls to hotel voice mail. I'm exhausted and getting hoarse. I decide to walk to the Reina Sofia, which is a museum I read about in my Madrid guidebook that is just south of El Retiro. I know I should go to the Prado first—that's like the really big museum here—but (1) it's overwhelmingly large, and (2) I don't like museums. I know that's not okay to admit if you want to be considered worldly and smart, but it's true. Museums make my back hurt because you have to stand for so long and move so slowly.

I make an on-the-go playlist that I label "Museum" on my iPod, and I set out to experience some culture. The music helps as I stare at the art—some paintings I even recognize, which means they must be really, really famous. I can't stop looking at this one by Picasso called *Guernica*. It's a scene of total chaos, and I read in the description that it's about the Spanish Civil War. Set to the Scissor Sisters' pulsing beats, I can't help thinking that it looks like the backstage area of a Fashion Week show where everyone's grabbing clothes and getting trampled, but I decide that's one of those too-shallow-to-share observations.

When I get back to the hotel, the red light on my phone is lit. I check for messages and hear that there are twenty-six in my inbox. As I start to listen to them, I realize that some of these people have already talked to the reporters I talked to.

"Is it true that you told the *Chicago Tribune* that you're taking a stand against the skinny aesthetic?" "Did you tell the *Oregonian* that you won't walk a runway alongside underweight models?" "Can you confirm that you said every single model you know has an eating disorder?"

Maybe it wasn't such a good idea to hold my own private press conference this morning. As I listen to each message, I feel a knot form in the pit of my stomach—and I start to see my modeling career flash before my eyes.

fifteen

       I have nonstop fittings from morning til night today, and I'm kind of glad. I'm running all around the city, so I hardly have time to worry about the interviews I gave yesterday, and I don't have to see Angela. Thank God.

But it's still not the greatest of days. I go through the motions of being stuck with pins and pinched by tape measures as usual, but this time I notice a little more frustration in the sighs of the people fitting me.

"What is it?" I quietly ask the tiny woman who's trying to get me into a fitted pantsuit.

"*Nada, gordita,*" she says, waving her tomato-shaped pin cushion.

Now I went pretty far in high school Spanish, and I don't remember *gordita* being pet-name slang. I'm pretty sure there's one translation: "little fat girl." Ouch.

For the rest of the day, I am positive that everyone who has to fit me is whispering under their breath about what a lard ass I am and how they can't believe I was cast in a single show. When I get back to the hotel at nine P.M., I fall onto my bed, close to tears. I turn on the TV and watch an *ER* rerun in Spanish.

I kind of hate myself for being so sensitive about this weight thing. I mean, I just told like a dozen reporters that I was standing up for girls and not bowing to the pressures of this thin-worshipping industry. But here I am, curled in a fetal ball on my hotel bed, hoping I'll fall asleep before I get hungry. Hoping I won't have to eat again tonight so I can fit into my clothes tomorrow. Hoping I'm not the laughingstock of Spain this weekend at the shows.

Brrring-brring. I can't bring myself to pick up the phone so I let it ring. When it gets close to midnight, I close the curtains and crawl into bed without dinner.

The next morning, my knees almost buckle when I take a shower, so I know I need something to eat. I start the day with an apple and a $9 Diet Coke from the minibar. I pull on a lightweight tank top and T-shirt, plus a black hooded sweatshirt and loose jeans. Layering always helps me feel hidden, and I definitely want to hide today. Too bad it's a runway day so that's impossible. I head downstairs with my sunglasses on. I don't want Angela to see my puffy eyes.

"Well, look who it is," says Angela, gesticulating wildly as I walk down the wide marble staircase to the lobby, where she's standing in front of a large planter filled with ferns and pink flowers. "It's the Voice of New Models."

I approach her warily. I can tell that she's upset with me, but she's being grandly sarcastic, so I wonder if she's half joking. I notice that she's holding several newspapers under her arm. *Uh-oh.*

"Did you think, my dear, that your giving quotes to the biggest newspapers in the United States would escape my notice?" Angela asks, in a fake sweet tone that tells me immediately that she is definitely not half joking. She's deadly serious. And definitely pissed.

"Angela, I—" I tentatively start to defend myself, but I realize there's no real way to do that. So I close my mouth.

"They're calling you *la gordita*," says Angela, holding up a copy of a Spanish newspaper that must have picked up my quotes. I raise my sunglasses to browse the headlines—she has five papers with her—which, if my high school Spanish is holding up, say that I'm speaking out against too-thin models and calling for a new consciousness in the industry.

"Charming, isn't it?" says Angela. She's more enraged than I've ever seen her, like a teapot whistling to a boil, and I'm almost scared she's going to physically strike me at any moment. "What exactly made you think you had the authority to speak out about any of this?"

"I just—"

"Uh-uh," says Angela, wagging her finger. "I'm not interested in your response. There is no excuse."

I pull down my sunglasses again to hide the tears that are forming in the corners of my eyes.

"We will finish the shows that you've booked here," Angela whispers angrily, under her breath. "And then you will go home. I may or may not make attempts to salvage your career."

"But I didn't—" I try again. She raises her hand in a *stop* gesture and marches out to the car that's waiting to take us to the shows. I follow her, deflated. Part of me hopes that she's overreacting, that the fashion world will embrace what I've said. But another part of me knows that Angela is right. I've really messed up this time.

As I dress for my first show, I can hear it: the quiet condemnation that's all around me. I can feel it while the makeup artist glitters my face up for a butterfly look at the Thomas Patrón show, I can feel it as a dresser helps me pull up my super suck-in tights for the Rocío show, and I can feel it when I walk out in the pantsuit at the Jorge Maldrón show and the flashbulbs erupt from the photographers' pit, along with screams of "*Viva, gordita!*" They don't want photos of the clothes—they want photos of the fat model who shot her mouth off about the fashion industry.

Backstage, I hear the other models whispering about me. Their eyes are boring into me, these girls who have long aspired to be the thinnest living beings on earth. And now I'm speaking out against them when I'm supposed to be one of them.

As I walk back to the car at the end of a long day, head down, shoulders slouched, I hear photographers yelling at me to turn around. "*Violeta, gordita! Una foto, por favor!*" Tears pool in my eyes as I shrink more into my hooded sweatshirt and turn up my iPod so I don't hear them. I duck into the back of the car and close my eyes for the ride to the hotel.

The next few days aren't any better. My interviews have been picked up all over Spain, and they're especially timely because it's Fashion Week. I talk to my parents on the phone—they've seen my quotes and are proud of what I said. I don't have the heart to tell them I'm not strong enough to follow through with being the new voice of models. I've been eating less and less each day.

Veronica and Sam have both called me to talk. They've tried to tell me it's okay, that the press will blow over, but I can hear in their voices that they're not sure what to say. I've broken an unspoken rule, the one where we all say we've got fast metabolisms and are genetically blessed. For many of us—like me—it's true. But to maintain a size 0–2, even the thinnest of us have to take some extreme measures. That's the part we're not supposed to mention. Especially not to the media.

When I finally reach Julie on the phone, I'm emotionally drained. It's my last night in Spain, the night before I should be heading to Milan. But Angela has canceled all of my Italian go-sees. She's decided not to drop me, but she wants me to lie low this season, to forget Milan and Paris.

"So what are you going to do?" Julie asks.

"I'm going home," I say. "What else is there to do?"

"You're going home to sit on the couch again like you did after the Paulo drama?" says Julie disapprovingly. "I don't know, Vi."

"Watching back-to-back *Made* episodes is so preferable to dealing with this crap," I say. "I just want to curl up in my comfort zone. Besides, it's not like I'm going to stay in Spain." And as I say it, I think to myself, *Why not stay in Spain?*

"Why not?" says Julie, echoing my thoughts.

I pause. *Could I?* "I've got some money saved," I say, starting to perk up. "My ticket is changeable."

"You're golden!" says Julie.

"I'm sure Mom and Dad would support a little travel," I continue, convincing myself.

"And you could stay in hostels and take trains around the country to see different cities!" says Julie giddily.

"Will you come out?" I ask, getting incredibly psyched at the idea of traipsing around Spain for a few weeks. Somehow in the midst of this fashion world angst, I'd forgotten why I got back into this modeling madness. *For the travel.* Well, modeling got me to Spain, and now it's time to experience this country on my terms. I can imagine nothing better than doing that with my best friend.

"Oh, Violet," says Julie, her excitement waning. "I wish I could. But I just started classes and I'm running for dorm vice president and I'm trying to worm my way onto the newspaper staff by doing a ton of grunt work for the editor in chief . . ."

"Okay, okay, overachiever," I say. I can't really blame Julie for being the way she's been all her life. I guess I didn't really think she'd drop everything to travel around Spain with me, like, tomorrow.

When we hang up, Julie's almost convinced me that it's better for me to travel alone anyway. That way, I can have my *Before Sunrise* moment, where I meet a young Ethan Hawke type on a train and fall madly in love with him. I'm conveniently ignoring the it-only-lasts-twenty-four-hours-and-I-never-see-him-again part.

But the truth is, I'm chicken. And as much as I want to be brave enough do this solo-in-Spain thing, I find myself dialing Roger's number soon after I hang up with Julie. Because there's not much of a chance, but . . .

"Señorita Greenfield," says Roger as he picks up his cell. "To what do I owe this honor?"

I feel a rush of warmth at the sound of his voice. We've IMed a lot while all this crazy stuff's been happening with the press, but I haven't actually spoken to Roger since I was in New York. Was that really just a week ago?

"Roger, hi—" I say. I'm surprised to find I'm slightly tongue-tied. "Listen, I had this crazy thought, and it's really last-minute and I'm sure you won't be able to—"

"Whoa, Speed Racer," he says. "What are you talking about?"

"Um, wanna meet me in Spain tomorrow?" I blurt out. Then I backtrack, and tell him about how Angela wants me to go home and forget Milan and Paris, and I've accepted that but I don't want to go home yet—I want to see more of the world while I'm here and well, it'd be fun to see it with him.

He doesn't respond.

"Roger?" I ask, wondering if we've lost our connection and I'm just rambling on and on for nothing.

"I'll be there," he says into the phone.

And my heart skips a beat.

sixteen

The next day, I'm sitting on top of a bunk bed in a definite hostel. I've never been in a hostel before, and I've been spoiled by the boutique hotels in São Paulo and Madrid. But Angela left this morning and I told her I was going to travel in Spain for a little while. She grunted and advised me to stay off MySpace and avoid reporters.

That's when I took my rolling suitcase and walked out of the posh hotel and around the corner to the Sonrisa Hostel. I got a teensy room that shares a bathroom with like ten other people. But at least Roger and I will have our own room, and I have to admit I was relieved to see the beds are bunked.

As I lie on the top bunk, waiting for Roger to get here—his flight landed an hour ago—I start to feel nervous. Why would Roger fly across the ocean on a moment's notice to hang out with me in Spain? He's missing a ton of classes, he hates airplanes, and he took Latin in high school, so it's not like he's going to brush up on his language skills. But I did ask him to come. Maybe he just knows how much I need him right now.

"Did somebody call a best friend in shining armor?" I hear Roger's voice from below and I sit straight up on the bunk, knocking my freakishly tall head on the ceiling.

"Ow!" I yell, but I look at Roger and see that he's trying not to laugh, which makes me giggle, and then we're both cracking up. I jump down to hug him as he drops his giant backpack. I lean in and my cheek touches his, which is stubbly but warm, and he smells like home, which makes my heart flutter. When I pull away I have to remind myself—it's just *Roger*. I must be more homesick than I thought.

"Nice backpack, Mr. Semi-Beard," I say.

"Yeah, well, you gotta do it right," he says. "I need a rugged five o'clock shadow and the ultimate traveler's pack if I'm going to run around Spain with a supermodel."

"Ugh—ex-supermodel, you mean," I say, sinking down onto the bottom bunk.

"Well, let's just say, supermodel-on-a-break," says Roger, joining me on the paper-thin cotton sheets.

"Yeah," I say quietly. "Let's make a rule: no model talk. I just want to be Roger and Violet for the next few days."

"Model? Who's a model?" says Roger. "Hey, doesn't this place remind you of home in New York, though?"

I laugh. Roger came to visit me at the model apartment last year, so he saw the *Zoolander*-esque setup we had where, Veronica, Sam, and I shared two bunk beds in one room. Come to think of it, I kind of *have* had the hostel experience before.

"No more fancy hotels for me," I lament. But as soon as the words are out of my mouth, I realize that I'm glad to be out of my Tryst ivory tower. Now I get to experience Europe like a normal eighteen-year-old! I'll be staying in hostels, meeting other travelers, cramming five museums into one afternoon. And all with a big-backpacked best friend at my side.

I smile at Roger and squeeze his hand. "So what do you want to do first?" I ask.

Over the next two days, Roger fills my hours with more culture than I've crammed into my whole life up to this point. We hit museums, historical tours, a tiny flamenco café he read about in the obscure travel books he brought with him—he's like a walking insider's guide to Madrid.

On the night before we wake up at six A.M. to take a train to Barcelona, I can tell I'm feeling the effects of the sangria when I lean in to give Roger a kiss on the cheek before I climb into the top bed. "You're the best," I say.

"Back atcha," says Roger, smiling.

When we lie down in our respective bunks, I want to keep talking. "Roger, do you think Chloe will be mad that you're traveling with me here?"

"I don't think Chloe will care," he says.

"And why's that?" I ask.

"Because Chloe knows we're old friends, Violet," says Roger. "It's not like she'd be jealous."

"Oh, right," I say, realizing that I was hoping for a different answer. I was hoping Chloe wasn't around anymore. But that's only because she's super annoying and not nearly good enough for Roger. You're not allowed to tell your friends that they're dating lame-os, though. It certainly didn't help last year when Roger called Peter Heller a douchebag and told me I was wasting my time with him. That only made me mad at Roger, as unfair as it may be.

"So tomorrow in Barcelona—I've got the afternoon planned out," says Roger, starting his nightly rundown of what we'll do the next day. As I listen to him talk excitedly about how beautiful he's heard the architecture is in Barcelona, and how we have to walk down a series of streets called Las Ramblas where everyone sells flowers and poetry, I interject a "Sounds fun," or "That would be great," where appropriate to show that I'm listening. And I am listening, right up until the point where I fall asleep to Roger's enthusiastic voice, which is one of the most comforting sounds in the world.

On the train ride to Barcelona, Roger and I score two seats facing each other so we can both sit next to the window.

"Phew," I say as we plop down. "I'm glad there wasn't a window-seat rematch there." When we were ten years old, Roger and I flew together to visit Julie for a week at her aunt's farm in Illinois over the summer. I was booked in the middle seat next to Roger's window, and we had an all-out war to decide who was going to get the prized seat-with-a-view. In the end, Roger let me have it, but only because I wouldn't stop singing the chorus from the Backstreet Boys' "I Want It That Way" until I got what I wanted. Roger got back at me by convincing me that Julie's aunt *really* needed me to get up before dawn and feed the pigs one morning. I reeked for days.

"I would have won this time," says Roger, smiling. "I'm immune to your awful singing now."

"Tell me whyeee . . ." I sing, imitating Nick Carter circa 1999.

"You are my fire," says Roger, deadpan.

"Believe . . . when I say," I reply. I love talking in song lyrics. Roger and I have this game where we keep repeating lyrics until one of us can't think of any more—and that person loses.

Roger looks down, silent.

"Giving up already?" I tease. "You lose if you can't think of another lyric."

"I guess I lose then," says Roger, turning to look out the window as the train starts to roll.

"You used to be much better at this game," I say. Roger is so weird. I know he knows more Backstreet Boys than that, but he's giving up. In fact, he seems suddenly sad.

"Hey, are you okay?" I ask.

"Just fine," he says, not looking away from the Spanish landscape that's rushing by us now.

"Well, I think you should be better than fine," I say, opening up my bag to grab a granola bar. I hold out the peanut-butter-flavored one to Roger because I know it's his favorite. He takes it grudgingly.

"And why is that?" he asks, still in a mood.

"Because you're on a train in Spain traveling with your best friend in the world," I say. "It's like a movie. And we're the stars. But of course we have a better script because our real-life banter is smarter than any Hollywood-invented lines."

I flash a winning smile as Roger turns to look at me.

"Yeah," he says, coming around. "But it might be a better movie if there were a love story element."

"Like *Before Sunrise*?" I ask, thinking about how Julie tried to persuade me to travel alone so I could meet my Ethan Hawke.

"Exactly," says Roger.

I sigh and lean back onto my fleece, which I've balled up as a pillow against the window. "Now you've brought me down," I say. "I wish Paulo were here."

"Oh, Violet, don't make me puke," says Roger, curling his lip in disgust. "Are you really thinking about that asshole right now?"

"Well you're the one who brought up Chloe and wishing *she* were traveling with you instead of me!" I snap at him.

"Chloe?!" says Roger. "When the hell did I bring up Chloe?"

"Just now, with all your talk about 'Blah, blah, this isn't fun because there's no romance,'" I say. "I mean, if you can't be apart from her for four days and enjoy the company of your oldest friend than I think you're really lame."

"What?" says Roger. "Okay, we're not talking about this anymore. And if you bring up Paulo again I swear I'm going to track him down and beat him up."

I smile a little at the thought of Roger beating *anyone* up.

"I will," he says, angrily. "Don't think I'm bluffing."

"Okay, Rocky Balboa," I say, laughing. "Let's just not fight any-more."

"I don't even know what we were fighting about!" says Roger, but I can see a smile playing on his lips and I know his bad mood is lifting as quickly as it came on.

For the rest of the train ride, we stare out at the countryside and talk about anything and everything—from the great TV I've missed since being abroad to Roger's theories on New York versus L.A., which I tease him endlessly for even proposing. I mean, as if he really has any idea—he's lived in New York for two seconds and he's never even *been* to L.A. It kind of is like *Before Sunrise*, but without the awkwardness. Because after all, this is my best friend here.

seventeen

We sign in at the tidy, if tiny, hostel that Roger booked for us. We're sharing a private room with two twin beds that might as well be a double, they're pushed so close together. Roger and I share a "what are you gonna do?" look and drop our bags on the bed. Then we stroll out into the city. Roger keeps insisting that we have to see all the buildings by Gaudi, this famous Spanish architect who designs structures that look like fantastical mansions with lots of color—at least that's how they look in the brochure. I'm so tired, though, that I convince him that we should do all that tomorrow. Today, we should walk lazily down Las Ramblas and get a bite to eat at an open-air café.

It's a gorgeous sunny day, and I have to admit that Roger was right about this street: It's absolutely charming. Cobblestones, flower vendors, musicians. We stop at a corner where Roger asks a street poet to make up a verse about us, and he writes it down on a lovely piece of pale yellow paper with peach-colored flowers around the edges. We can't see what he's writing, and when he's done, he makes Roger hand him five hundred pesetas, which is like $4, before he'll turn over the verse.

No mas que amigos; no menos que amor verdadero, says the cursive script. "No more than friends; no less than true love," I translate. "Five hundred pesetas for one sentence?"

"Yeah," says Roger, shoving the paper into his back pocket. "Weird."

Eventually, we end up down by the port just as the sun is setting. The clouds are a bright pink, like Candyland clouds. "Hey, Violet," says Roger.

"What?"

"If God's not a Tarheel . . ." he starts.

"Then why's the sky Carolina blue?" I finish, completing a phrase that's on a bumper sticker I used to love when I was a kid—we've always been rabid college basketball fans.

We stare out at the sunset for another few minutes before deciding to have dinner at the restaurant on the pier. "My treat," I say. "I might as well use my modeling money for something fun before Dad makes me blow it all on tuition next semester."

"Yeah, let's do something really *useful* with it," says Roger. "Like eat a ton of seafood."

We order shrimp, squid, and olive-paste-covered tapas—which are small plates that are really popular here—and we get a huge pitcher of sangria. By the time we leave the restaurant, I'm feeling a little buzzed. "Wouldn't this be romantic if we were with, like, someone romantic?" I say, taking hold of Roger's hand as we walk down the pier. "I'm off balance," I explain, half joking, as I smile at him.

On the way back to the hostel, Roger makes me laugh by finding Spanish doppelgangers for people we know from home. When he points at a homely, rotund man pushing a cart and says, "Brian Radcliff," naming the guy I had a crush on all through high school, I double over in laughter. But as I stand back up, I surprise myself by starting to cry.

"Whoa, Violet," says Roger, grabbing my arm and pulling me to sit down on a nearby street bench. "I had no idea you were so hung up on that guy." He's smiling slightly—he knows that I'm over Brian Radcliff—but I can tell he's kind of nervous. He doesn't know what brought on the tears. And I'm not sure I do either.

"What is it?" asks Roger, softly rubbing my back.

"I don't know," I say, feeling silly and trying to wipe my tears with my thin shirt sleeve. "I just feel really sad all of a sudden." I'm thinking about the trouble I got in with Angela and the possibility that my modeling career is over, I'm thinking about people on snarky blogs who may be talking shit about me, I'm thinking about the fact that I deferred college—which feels like deferring my life— for a dream that isn't coming true. I tell Roger all that, and he nods sympathetically with every sentence.

But what I don't tell him is that my heart is still a little bit broken. I miss Paulo. It's impossible to be in this city and not wish you were holding hands with someone for real, kissing someone, going home with someone. I'm scared, though, that if I talk about Paulo, Roger will get mad again. He's so protective of me, I think, as I lift my head and look into his worried blue eyes. I smile and reach up to ruffle his hair, just to let him know that I'm okay.

And then I'm kissing him. Or he's kissing me. And a million thoughts are running through my head. *Am I kissing Roger? Is Roger kissing me? Is my hand in his hair? Are his hands cupping my face? Is this lasting for more than ten seconds? Are we making out?*

That's when I pull back.

"Roger!" I shout.

"Violet, I—" he starts.

Then I just look back at him and can't help it—I start to laugh. I'm giggling like crazy. I'm a little buzzed, I admit, but this situation is totally ridiculous. Roger is staring at me blankly.

Then suddenly, his face shifts, and he smiles too. "Yup," he says, "That's how old Roger gets the ladies out of a bad mood." He stands

up and holds out his hand. I grab it and we stumble down the cobblestone street, back to our hostel. Where we sleep back-to-back in
the almost-double bed.

The next morning, I wake up before Roger and jump into
the shared shower while it's free. There are six Australian travelers
in the big room next to us, so I want to get my hot water while I can.
As the steam pours over me, I think about last night. I'm not sure
how to feel about that kiss. It had to be a joke, right? A drunken
laugh gone a teensy bit too far. I remember being surprised at how
soft Roger's hair felt in my hands—it usually has gel in it but he's
been pretty *au naturel* since we've been traveling. Should I bring
anything up this morning? Play it off with a comment about his
weird ChapStick addiction? Even thinking about this is making me
feel uncomfortable—Roger's probably super embarrassed that it
happened. It was just one of those things—I was emotional, we'd
been drinking, there may have even been soft Spanish music playing,
I'm remembering now. And the moon was out over the water. I will
myself to push the scene from my mind—it's *Roger*, my best friend
from forever. Any confusion that kiss caused is only a sign that I'm
still hurting from the Paulo situation. I don't want this morning to be
awkward, so I'm just chalking it up to a bizarre evening with too
much sangria. There! I'm officially done thinking about it.

When I walk back in the room, Roger's awake and sitting up on
the bed in his "JESUS LOVE JEWS" T-shirt and dog-bone boxer shorts.

"Ready to see the great works of Señor Gaudí?" I ask, pulling
open the curtains and letting the sunshine in. "You've only got two
more days in Spain before you go back to New York."

"Uh, yeah," says Roger, squinting at the light.

"I think you have time to get in the shower before the Australians," I say. "Did you hear them coming in at like five A.M.?
Sounds like they had a wild night."

Roger looks down and pulls at a hangnail. "Violet?" he says, not looking up at me.

"Yes, gross nail-picker?" I say, sitting down next to him.

"About last night . . ." he starts.

"Roger, don't even mention it," I say, waving my hand as if to push all thoughts of The Kiss away. "It was silly. It was sangria. It was Spain. Hey, I just thought up that alliterative explanation. Pretty good, huh?" I smile at him, but he's not indulging my need to make the awkwardness go away. And I do realize I'm sounding desperately dorky in my attempts to stop him from talking about it.

"Well, yeah," he says. "But I was thinking that maybe I would stay longer. In Spain, I mean."

"Huh?" I ask, confused. "Your ticket's for Monday, right?"

"Uh-huh," says Roger. "But you know, I don't really need to go back." And then he launches into this big explanation of how he doesn't like his roommate and he chose the wrong classes and how nothing fits in New York. "I just feel like it would be better if I could start fresh next semester," he says. "So like I could take time off and we'd both be going to college in January."

"And in the meantime, we'd . . . ?" I ask.

"Buy a Eurorail pass!" says Roger, jumping up and pulling on his jeans. He has a huge smile on his face. "We'd go to Italy and France and Switzerland and Germany—though not in that order of course. I could show you a different Brian Radcliff in each country."

I laugh. Roger is on a roll.

"And we'd eat fine cheeses and drink the best wines that five dollars can buy. We'd go to Oktoberfest and—"

Brring, brring. My phone.

"Hold that thought, Carmen Sandiego," I say. As I rifle through my bag to find my cell, I think about what Roger's proposing. Traveling through Europe with my best friend doesn't sound like a bad way to spend the fall. Maybe Julie could even come out over October break and city-hop with us for a week.

I glance at the phone and see that the Caller ID is "unavailable." For a second I wonder if I should answer it—what is the rate for getting a call in a foreign country? I've barely used the phone at all, and no one back home has really even thought to call it. No one except . . .

"Hello?" I say into the phone.

"Vacationing Violet," says a familiar voice. Angela. I grimace. "Back in the States, are we?" she asks.

"Actually I'm in Bar—" I start.

"Not important, darling, just get to Paris," she orders.

"Paris?" I ask.

"Paris—the city of lights, the city of love, gay Paree!" she exclaims. "Someone's asking for you. Don't ask me why, don't ask me how, don't ask me who—yet. Just get yourself on a plane pronto. I'll have a car waiting for you at Charles de Gaulle Airport tonight. Ta."

And then she's gone.

"Who was that?" asks Roger.

"It was Paris," I whisper, visions of traveling with my best friend being swiftly replaced by the allure of the runway lights in the fashion capital of the world.

"Hilton?" says Roger, smiling. "I never answer her calls."

He doesn't get it. He doesn't realize this means that I have to go.

"It was Angela," I say. "I have to get a flight out of Barcelona."

"What?" says Roger. "What are you talking about? We were just making plans to—"

"Roger, this is my career," I say. "Paris is like the pinnacle."

"Please, Violet," he says, as he starts shoving clothes into his big backpack. "We're eighteen years old—this isn't life or death."

"Okay," I say, "But it *is* important to me."

"So you're just going to get on a plane, just like that," says Roger, staring at me angrily. "Angela snaps her fingers and you run to her side. After all the insults and threats she's hurled at you and the shitty way she's treated you."

"That's just what agents are like," I say softly, not really wanting to admit that I *am* kind of letting Angela dictate my life.

"God, you are such a fucking disappointment!" yells Roger, so loudly I'm sure everyone in this hostel with paper-thin walls can hear him. "I come here at the drop of a hat to make you happy, to save you from this bullshit fashion world you say you don't want any part of—and look at you. You must like the abuse—the way you say they make you feel fat when you're easily ten pounds underweight, the way they stare at you and talk about you like you're an inanimate object wearing their clothes, the way guys like Paulo cast you aside for next week's hottest model. Violet, can't you see you're being used?"

Roger looks at me pleadingly, and I want to agree with him—I do. Part of me knows that he's right—that last year I made a decision to leave the modeling world for good, and maybe I should have stuck with it. Then I would never have let Paulo hurt me, never have gotten into this trouble with the press, never have anguished over my body the way only runway models do. I'd be Violet Greenfield from Carolina, best friend of Roger and Julie, college student, all around good girl. But I'd also never have seen Brazil or Spain—or now France! I wouldn't know the thrill of the international runway. And maybe most important, I'd always wonder: what if? And that's how I feel about Paris right now.

My head is spinning. Someone important asked for me. Someone in *Paris* asked for me. And even though I've never seen my best friend this angry, I start packing my bag.

"I have to leave," I say firmly. "Tonight."

eighteen

On the plane to Paris, I'm trying to act normal as I order a Diet Coke and pick at my tiny bag of pretzels, but it's hard to pull off "normal" when a zillion emotions are rushing through your body. I feel guilty about Roger, who looked at me like I'd just killed his dog as I walked out of the hostel and hailed a cab to the airport. I feel conflicted because I was just getting into the idea of being a regular eighteen-year-old traveling with her best friend and staying in hostels and starting a normal life where I don't have to compete and backstab and practice insincerity to get ahead. And here's why I'm a hypocrite: because the second Angela said "Get to Paris," I felt a rush of excitement, a thrill that—sorry, Roger—a Eurorail pass just can't provide. I've been trying to talk myself out of the fashion world, but the truth is, I'm addicted to it. Violet Greenfield, Regular Girl just isn't as cool as Violet Greenfield, Supermodel. If I don't take this chance, I could go back to being the too-tall girl with bad posture who never had a date in high school. I can't let that happen.

When I get off the plane, I see a short, mustached man holding a whiteboard with my name on it. "Mademoiselle," he says, bowing.

"Hi," I say. "I'm Violet."

"And I am your driver tonight," he replies. "*Je m'appelle Pierre.*" I smile. That name is so stereotypically French that it would completely amuse Roger. And for a second I feel a pang as I think of him alone in the hostel tonight, and I wonder if he got to see all he wanted to in Barcelona today. I hope he found someone to hang out with—maybe the Australians from the hostel? I bite my lip. Oh, man, I'm such a bad friend.

But as Pierre helps me with my bags and leads me to a plush Town Car with leather seats and a bottle of Perrier chilled in the back for me, I can't help but lean back and sigh. This sure beats third class on the train to Barcelona.

I'm watching the sights of Paris flash by me—yellow twinkles on the Eiffel tower, tiny little cars driving alongside us, the beautiful stone buildings with old-fashioned shutters that look so charming. When we stop at a light, I see the black-and-gold iron gates of the city and the ornate, gothic streetlamps that light the sidewalks. Then, Pierre breaks my reverie.

"We will go straight to the party, mademoiselle," says Pierre.

"Pardon?" I say, sitting up straight.

"Miss Blythe has told me you are to be at the party as soon as you land," he says.

"Wait—what party?" I ask. Pierre shrugs at me in the rearview mirror as if to say, *Beats me*, just as my phone starts to ring.

"Reviving Violet," says Angela.

"Where am I going?" I ask.

"You're coming to the Hotel le Fleur, of course," she coos. "The eighth-floor ballroom. And please, wear something simple and elegant. If it's a fat week, wear something swingy. Oh, and pull that hair back into a bun."

"But where am I supposed to—?" I start to ask.

"Leave your luggage with the front desk, use the first-floor bathroom to primp and do not approach the elevator bank until you're party-ready," barks Angela. "I can't have people seeing you in your just-off-the-plane state. You haven't quite mastered the travel-chic look yet, darling." Then she laughs and hangs up the phone.

"And you haven't quite mastered the common courtesy of a good-bye," I whisper angrily into the phone.

"Pardon, mademoiselle?" ask Pierre.

"Oh, nothing," I say. "The Hotel le Fleur it is."

"*Oui*, mademoiselle," he replies. And we drive on through the streets of Paris, past the insane traffic pattern around the Arc d'Triomphe and on my way to a mystery party in the most fashionable city in the world. I look down at my drawstring cotton yoga pants and cringe. I hope I'm ready for this.

Under bright lights and in front of a gold-gilt mirror, I primp in a private stall of the hotel's first-floor bathroom. This place is *swank*. I put on a loose, forest-green jersey dress that never wrinkles and—I've been told—makes my eyes really pop. It's not the most fancy, but with a few gold bangles on my wrist, a triple-strand necklace and the most painful pair of high heels I own—the ones with jewels up and down the heel—I think it's dressy enough. I sweep my hair into a bun and tease the front a little bit to give it some volume—Sam taught me that move last year. Then I line my eyes with a gray charcoal pencil, sweep on some mascara and lipstick, and head for the elevator banks. Eighth-floor ballroom, here I come.

I take a deep breath as the doors open. In front of me are waiters carrying silver trays that hold tiny appetizers—shrimp bites and petit sandwiches and toothpick-speared varieties of cheese. I spy beautiful women in full-length couture gowns holding sparkling crystal flutes of champagne; I hear a string quartet in the corner playing classical music. I also see men in tuxedos smiling and winking at the models who are interspersed in the crowd, all looking more blank-faced and casual than the couture-wearing older women, I notice thankfully. And I see Angela's big, white smile coming right at me.

I step out of the elevator just before the doors close.

"Vivacious Violet," shouts Angela, obviously hoping to turn some heads with her volume. "You're a vision!" Then, more quietly, she whispers in my ear, "Good idea of mine, you wearing something loose—I see you didn't go hungry in your week off."

I feel a flash of shame as Angela taps into my body insecurities once again. I stare out into the ballroom, suddenly seeing all the models' arms—their elbows cocked to the side in a pose we're taught to do so that the sheer, jagged skinniness of our limbs will be on full display. I look down at my own arms, half hidden beneath the winged sleeves of my loose dress, and I'm glad that no one can see how pudgy they've gotten. But Angela always knows.

Before I can sink deeper into my world of insecurity, Angela grabs my arm and pulls me over to a circle of people. Actually, it's *the* circle of people—I can tell right away that these are the most glamorous guests in attendance. The way they laugh with their heads at full tilt, the way they hold their drinks with delicate fingers, the way one woman in particular keeps opening and closing a stunning silver-jeweled cigarette case with her perfect red fingernails, as if waiting for just the right moment to escape to the balcony for a smoke. *Wait—is that . . . ?*

Before I can finish my thought, Angela answers my half-formed question for me. "Violet, meet Mirabella Prince," says Angela, gesturing toward the cigarette-case woman, who I now notice is staring at me intently with her deep brown, almond-shaped eyes.

"Violet," she coos in a semi-French accent. "I've been waiting to see you."

And suddenly I realize that Mirabella Prince must be the one who called for me, the one who got Angela to take another chance on me even when I thought I was out of chances. And she's the only type of designer who could do it. Mirabella is the daughter of a famous filmmaker and a former supermodel; her show is always the biggest night in Paris. I've heard that even some celebrities are denied entrance because of the massive demand for tickets. I think even my brother, Jake—who could give a shit about the fashion world—knows her name. She is Big-Time.

"Very nice to meet you, Ms. Prince," I manage to say.

"Come," she says, putting a snow-white hand around my shoulder and leading me away from the group before I have a chance to say hello to any of the others. "Walk with me."

She leads me outside to the balcony, where there is a view of the sparkling Eiffel Tower in the distance. I feel a tingle run through me, though I haven't had a glass of champagne yet. I am in *Paris*! I walk slowly out onto the terrace and place my hands on the stone edge to steady their shaking. I don't want to seem like a nervous freak in front of Mirabella Prince. She looks at me kindly, though, and smiles.

"Violet," she murmurs softly. "I love what you said on the Internet. I love what you said to the newspapers. I love what you stand for."

"Oh, thank you," I say, not quite sure what to make of her compliments.

"It is true that you all are not just fashion models, but also role models for young girls, especially when it comes to a positive body image," she continues. "You know that, and you have spoken from your heart about the subject."

I nod, suddenly feeling pretty good about the convictions that landed me in trouble with Angela.

"And that's why I want you to close my show this year," says Mirabella Prince, turning her head to the side and blowing smoke around my face. "You'll convey to the world that I too am conscientious and caring. I too worry about the impression we're making on young girls who love fashion."

"Oh, I'm so glad you feel that way, Ms. Prince," I gush, completely excited about the possibility of being able to walk a runway without worrying about an extra five pounds or whether the girls on MySpace will see me and start starving themselves to emulate an impossible ideal. This could be my perfect moment—standing strong in something I really believe in and up on a runway. The biggest runway in Paris, no less. "I won't let you down. I've always loved your clothes—not that I could afford them, but my best friend Julie and I flip through magazines and whenever we see your new designs we just freak out. I mean in a good way, Ms. Prince, because we—"

I guess I'm rambling because she finishes her cigarette and puts her finger to her mouth, gently shushing me while ushering me back inside. "Call me Mirabella," she purrs.

For the rest of the night I feel like I'm watching my life from above as Angela introduces me to some of the biggest names in fashion. They all seem to know that I'll be walking Mirabella Prince's show—and they're practically salivating over me. Apparently, Mirabella made a deal with Angela that I will appear in her show and her show only, so even though I am walking once, I'm earning like ten times the norm for this job so that she has exclusive rights to me. Suh-weet.

When Angela and I fall into the back seat of the Town Car at the end of the night, I sigh a giddy sigh. I also can't help but savor the I-told-you-so moment.

"So I guess it was my MySpace posts and those newspaper interviews that got me the Mirabella Prince show, right?" I ask, trying to sound casual.

"I suppose so," says Angela, checking her Treo without looking up at me.

"Umm-hmm," I hum, sitting back in satisfaction.

"Oh, Violet," says Angela, lifting her head and smiling slightly. "Before I forget—Mirabella did ask me to tell you that you'll have to lose five pounds before the show."

"What?" I whisper, dumbfounded.

"Aw, dear," says Angela. "Well, she didn't want to mention it to-night with all the excitement, but you will need to fit into her sample size—we don't want any ripped seams, of course. Chorizo and chur-ros can be such a tempting treat while you're in Spain, but the vaca-tion's over, little lamb."

"But what about the things she said?" I ask, almost to myself. "About being a role model for girls and having a positive body image and—"

"Don't worry about that, my dear," says Angela. "Remember, the camera adds ten pounds, so you'll look all right to the girls at home."

I sink back in my seat, feeling utterly beaten down and deflated.

"Why so sad, Violet?" asks Angela. "Mirabella loves your PR work, she just wants you to lose five pounds. You're okay in the slouchy dress, but her clothes under the glare of those runway lights are unforgiving."

I feel a tear trickle down my cheek as we pull up to our hotel.

"Don't embarrass me, Violet," says Angela, suddenly stern as she steps out of the car. "Just lose the five pounds."

I'm too upset to talk to Angela right now, so I head for the front desk to get my key. I need to be alone. I look back at her as she boards the elevator. Then she turns her head in my direction.

"Oh, and Virtual Violet?" she says. "Don't even think about blogging this."

Then with a ding of the elevator doors, she's gone. And I'm dev-astated.

nineteen

I wake up the next morning with a crying headache. I look around at my beautiful suite—complete with gigantoid living room and glorious views of a beautiful courtyard patio four floors below—and I wonder just who is paying for all this. It can't be Tryst. There's even a huge bouquet of deep purple violets on the entryway table. I put on the ivory-colored silk slippers that are sitting at my bedside and shuffle over to the flowers. The card reads:

Violets for my new muse. Let's make girls feel beautiful in their own skin. *Un bizou*, Mirabella

Her name is scrawled in elegant, loopy penmanship. And that's when I realize I've been totally bought and paid for.

I am in one of those moments where I imagine myself going really insane. I have an urge to tear the card in half and smash the violets' vase on the floor, right before I rip the floor-to-ceiling curtains from their rods, knock the fruit bowl off its marble-top table perch, and karate chop the four-poster bed into little pieces of firewood. In real life, I just put the card on the table, sit down on the divan by the window, and start crying again.

If I do this Mirabella show, it could *make* my career. She'll get a ton of great publicity for using me—she'll seem really progressive and pro-girl—and I'll get to have a platform for voicing my opinions about how projecting a positive body image, even in the modeling world, is essential. But it'll all be a sham. I'll have to lose five pounds in three days before the show, which means starving myself and screwing up my metabolism for a quick fix, and I'll walk the runway knowing that Mirabella is a big fat liar. Or a scarily skinny liar, but whatever—a fraud either way.

Suddenly, my phone lights up with a text message. Veronica! It reads, "in paris. meet me @ musee rodin, 2pm." She's in town! Thank God.

I jump in the shower and attempt to depuff my cried-out eyes with some of the fancy hotel creams. Then I get dressed and head downstairs to ask the concierge what exactly "musee rodin" means—and where I can find it.

The Rodin Museum, which is at the Hotel Biron, has an amazing garden. When I arrive, I feel like I should go inside and see some of the exhibit, but it's such a sunny day that I decide to just enjoy the elegant outdoor space and wait for Veronica. Besides, some of Rodin's sculptures are out there, so it totally counts as a museum trip. Well, in my book it does.

I scan the grounds for Veronica, but I don't see her, so I sit down on a bench between two really well-groomed bushes that are taller than I am. I have to admit—this place is absolutely gorgeous. I even recognize a sculpture—*The Thinker*—and I snap a picture with my phone so I can impress Roger later by proving I did something cultural while I was in Paris, even without him by my side. That is, if he's speaking to me after I stranded him. I sigh.

All around me I see the romance of Paris, couples sharing loving glances and walking hand in hand—even some of the statues in this place are making out. I sigh. Why did Paulo have to mess around with that Skinnyskank girl? I think back to the first night when we drove in his car and he told me how he'd rescued her from a rusty heap and named her Gracie. How can any guy who talks so lovingly about an old car be such a jerk? And how can I possibly miss such a jerk this much?

Just as this thought flashes through my mind, I hear a familiar voice.

"V!" screams Veronica.

"V!" I yell back, standing up and giving her a hug while jumping up and down. "I am so, so happy to see you!"

"Likewise," she says, breaking my bouncing hug and cocking her head to one side to look me up and down.

"Don't say it—" I immediately snap. "I know I need to lose five pounds."

"Did you insult her already, Veronica?!" says an Australian voice from behind me.

"Sam!" I shout, spinning around to give my other ex-roommate a hug. "You guys are *both* here?"

"Duh, it's Paris!" says Veronica. "*Everyone* is here."

"And you guys are, like, hanging out?" I ask cautiously. "You're friends?"

"Friends, frenemies," says Sam, smiling. "It's all the same in this industry."

Veronica laughs and I can tell that she and Sam have become closer. "We were together in Milan," says Sam. "We bonded when Veronica slapped some jerk who pinched my ass."

"Another friendship built on butt-guarding," says Veronica, smiling.

"I'm so glad," I say. "Because I need both of your advice."

"What is it?" asks Sam, looking concerned.

"Is it the stuff that happened with the press?" asks Veronica.

"Let's sit down," I say, pulling them onto the bench with me. "We've got a lot to talk about."

I give Veronica and Sam the backstory on the whole MySpace debacle and how the press just got out of control, at least from my perspective. They nod supportively but don't say anything—I know they can tell I need to get everything out before they comment. I skip over Roger and The Kiss and all that because it's so not worth mentioning. But when I talk about last night's party with Mirabella Prince, I give them every detail—how she hired me for her show exclusively, how she praised my stance on positive body image, and how she had Angela tell me I needed to drop five pounds before I can walk her runway.

And then I wait for their jaws to drop, for Sam and Veronica to stand up and shout indignantly about what a phony Mirabella is and how wrong it would be if I crash-dieted before walking a runway in the name of being a good role model.

But neither jaw drops. And neither of my friends stands up. They just look at me with wide eyes, waiting to hear more.

"Well, that's it," I say. "That's the problem. What should I do?"

"Wait—" says Sam. "*What's* the problem exactly?"

"Yeah," says Veronica. "I mean, if it's the five pounds I can totally help you out with that."

"What?" I say, dumbfounded. "No—I mean—the five pounds isn't the problem!"

"So . . . ?" says Sam, looking genuinely confused.

"Helloooo!" I shout, standing up and facing their confused faces as they sit on the bench. "The *problem* is that walking in this show under these pretenses makes me a hypocrite! If Mirabella's going to sell her line with the message that she's into healthy bodies and self-confident girls, then she shouldn't be asking her closing model to lose five pounds before the freaking show!" I realize I'm screaming now, and the other patrons of the garden, who probably enjoy a little silence with their pink roses and priceless works of art, are staring at me.

I sit back down on the bench. *Sorry*, I mouth to one sourpuss old lady giving me the eye.

I catch Veronica and Sam shrugging at each other nervously.

"Listen, Violet," says Veronica. "I know you're into this whole 'girl power message' thing—"

"Oh, God, please no air quotes," I say, exasperated. "And never say *girl power* again."

"Sorry," says Veronica.

"It's okay," I say. "Go on."

"So this message thing," she says. "It's cool and I think it's great that you want to do something positive for girls—"

"Although we were a little miffed to read the part about how every single model you know has an eating disorder," says Sam, chiming in.

"Yeah, I know," I say. "I realized that was kind of overstepping."

"Some of us really do have fast metabolisms," says Sam.

Veronica and I look at each other and laugh. "Like who?" I say.

"Well . . . those girls from . . . I'm sure there's someone who . . ." Sam looks at us and starts to laugh herself. "Oh I don't know! Okay, go on, Veronica."

"Anyway, a few exceptions aside, I think we all read your quotes and agreed with you that girls shouldn't be comparing themselves to the standard of beauty that models are expected to keep up with," continues Veronica. "But you have to remember—the reality of the industry is that thin is in right now. Being a waif is how you book jobs. Besides, the whole positive-body-image thing is a great platform for you to get some more exposure, but you don't actually have to live your life by it."

"Yeah," says Sam. "And really, five pounds is nothing."

I shake my head, wondering how I can get them to understand. "But in an ideal world," I say, "I'd *want* to live my life by the message I'm conveying."

"Yeah, well it's not an ideal world," says Veronica. "It's the modeling world. And Mirabella Prince is about as big a show as you can land."

"It's true," says Sam. "I suggest you do whatever it takes to walk it."

I consider what they've said, and a few minutes later—after we've strolled through the lushly manicured garden and back onto the bustling Parisian street—I've made a decision. Like I told Roger, this is my career. It's important to me.

I turn to Veronica. "So how do you lose five pounds in three days?" I ask.

twenty

I am justifying my breakfast of half a banana (and my lunch of the other half of the banana) by pretending I'm sick. When you're sick, you can't eat much. And besides, not eating much makes me feel sick, so it's not that much of a stretch.

Veronica and Sam have outlined what I can and can't eat for the next two days. They both have constant fittings, though, so I have to get through this without their support. I really, really want to blog about everything, but I know that's dangerous. I'm proud of myself because I haven't even gone online once since I've been in Paris—I feel like it always gets me into trouble. Besides, Angela keeps complaining about how French hotels never have good Internet connections, so it's probably not worth the hassle.

I sit down with a pen and paper to write a letter to Julie. I haven't talked to her in like a week—I think she's probably really busy with her college overachievement plan. Shouldn't she be able to let up? I mean, she got in already—relax! When I asked her about slowing down, she said, "Violet, prospective employers and grad school admissions officers want to see that you made the most of your four years in school." Typical Julie.

I start to write the letter, but when I reveal that I'm basically not eating for a couple of days, I realize I can't send it. This is more journal-entry material. I read the letter back to myself, and when I get to the part about how I feel lonely sitting in this big, empty suite with just French TV and the minibar key (which is taunting me), I realize I'm being ridiculous. Any girl from my high school—or from any high school for that matter—would kill to be in my shoes. I'm getting paid to be in Paris and stay at one of the best hotels in the city—in a suite, no less! How can I possibly be upset? I push my conflicted feelings to the back of my mind and strengthen my resolve to (1) enjoy the city, (2) lose five pounds, and (3) stop thinking about Paulo. The truth is, Paulo has re-entered my thoughts with a vengeance. It must be something about Paris, something about its romantic energy that takes me back to those summer-like days in the pool house. And, not to think in *Grease* songs, but oh, those summer nights. Ugh—there I go again!

I write a postcard to my parents and Jake so I can clear my head. I tell them about Mirabella's show (but not about the conflicting messages), how Roger and I had fun in Barcelona (but not about The Kiss), and how Veronica and Sam are both here (but not about how they're helping me lose weight). So I tell them everything, but also nothing.

Knock, knock.

Finally! Veronica and Sam are coming over for "dinner." We're going to order room service to the suite so we can watch what I'm eating and not feel self-conscious at a restaurant. It's Veronica's idea.

I open the door and am immediately blinded by a bright flashbulb. I put my hand up to block the light and I see an extremely short man with a huge camera standing just three feet in front of me.

"Um, who are you?" I ask, sounding meeker than I mean to. I mean to sound angry, which I am.

But the man doesn't answer. He just flashes his camera a few more times and then takes off running down the hall. Then I see Veronica and Sam coming from the other direction.

"Did you guys just see that?!" I yell.

"What?" says Sam, looking down and studying her newly manicured nails. "My new French tips? Aren't they divine?" She holds up her hand for me to see.

"Not your nails! That freak who took my picture!" I say. "He was just standing outside my door!"

"Oh, God," says Veronica. "It's the French paparazzi. Jesus, I thought this whole celebrity culture thing was dying down."

"Celebrity culture?" I ask. "It's not like I'm Victoria Beckham over here."

"Yeah, but European gossip rags will run even D-listers like you, Greenfield," says Veronica. And though I know she meant it as a joking insult, I'm kind of thrilled to think of myself as a D-lister. But I'm not so thrilled that there was just a strange man outside my door.

"Forget about it," says Sam as she and Veronica walk inside the suite and look around. "Now *this* is what I'm talking about."

"Mirabella Price spares no expense," says Veronica. A couple of years back, Veronica was the one walking Mirabella's show. I wonder if she's mad at me for taking her place this year.

"Don't sweat it, V," says Veronica, noticing my tense face. "I'm not jealous—Mirabella's kind of a cow to work with. This year is so much more low-key for me, and I'm enjoying it. Besides, I still get to dine in this suite, don't I?"

"Anytime!" I say, trying not to overreact about the photographer who just totally violated my personal space. "Let's look at the menu."

For my meal, Sam and Veronica choose a bunch of *à la carte* things, which Sam says translates to "from the menu" but in reality it's a whole bunch of things that are *not* from the menu. More like things we'd like involving ingredients they have—meals that are loosely based on what's listed. So I get a plate of steamed vegetables and a quarter fillet of salmon, while Veronica gets a bunless burger and Sam orders the steak frites. "We're *not* trying to lose two pounds a day," they explain when I pout.

I'm kind of proud of myself for only eating a banana so far, but Veronica and Sam told me I'd be rewarded for my self-control at dinner, and this veggies-and-fish combo just isn't cutting it.

"There's no flavor!" I whine.

"It's two days, Violet," says Sam patiently. "Suck it up. And if you don't like what you got, don't eat it. That's within the rules."

When we roll the room service tray back out into the hall, it still has half my plate of fish and vegetables on it. And I am still hungry.

The whole next day is a blur of sitting on my suite's divan and watching bad French television. I want to go out and enjoy the city, but I feel so lethargic that I just stay in, drinking $20 bottles of Perrier from the minibar and allowing myself a squirt of lemon to make them taste better. Roger used to always crush up lemons into his water when he was too cheap to spring for a drink. "Instant lemonade is so refreshing!" he'd say, taking a sip. I laugh out loud at the memory, and I realize I must be hallucinating.

On day three, though, I have the fitting for Mirabella. Veronica says I'll be able to eat normally again tomorrow. As long as I make it through the fitting, I'm home free.

As an assistant measures my waist, I suck in tightly and try to read her face for signs of disapproval. She looks up at me and smiles, "*C'est parfait!*" she says, motioning to someone around the corner. Two men walk in carrying a long, gold gown. And I do mean *gold*. They are having trouble holding it straight, I notice.

"Is it heavy?" I ask the assistant.

She looks up at me and nods. "Forty pounds," she says.

My jaw drops. The irony of my just having killed myself to lose five pounds when I'm about to add forty to my frame is not lost on me. But after they manage to build the dress around my body, I realize that this gown—which is made of real metal interwoven with fabric—is skintight, terribly heavy, and devastatingly gorgeous.

Suddenly, there's a flutter of activity and Mirabella walks into the fitting room. When she sees me, she inhales dramatically, clasping her hands to her chest. Is that a tear I see in her eye? She rushes over and hovers around me, scanning my silhouette from all angles.

"Violet, you are stunning," she says. "You are the Statue of Liberty, the Eiffel Tower, the absolute beacon of Paris fashion in this dress!"

I gaze into the mirror along the side wall and—though I don't tear up like Mirabella does—I do feel a rush of energy at seeing myself in this dress. It is hands down the most beautiful piece of clothing I've ever seen—let alone worn. Although it's undeniably gold, it shimmers when the light hits it, kind of like the mica in rocks that Roger and Julie and I used to pick up in my backyard. The colors it reflects range from pink to peach to coral, and the way it drapes heavily down to the ground makes it look like it could be a gown from a classical painting of a Greek goddess.

"I love it," I say to Mirabella.

"Obviously," she replies, and I realize her emotional moment has ended as quickly as it began. "You know you're in the running for being the next face of Mirabella Prince."

"You mean the campaign?" I ask. It would be an incredible score to pose for Mirabella Prince ads—maybe even bigger than the Voile campaign.

"Yes," says Mirabella. "And you're right. It is *the* campaign. Now: walk."

After two hours of working on my impeded stride in the most-beautiful-but-heaviest-dress-ever, I'm exhausted. I push open the double doors and burst outside, grateful that my short-shorts and lace top combo weighs less than one pound. I took a car to the fitting, but I think I'll be adventurous and take the Metro back to the hotel— I'll count it as another Paris experience for the books. On the way into the tunnel, I drop my parents' postcard in a mailbox and pick up a bottled water—the only thing I'll have consumed today.

I buy a ticket and board a train without incident, feeling pretty happy with myself for figuring out which direction to go in. But as soon as the Metro starts to move, I get a head rush. And not just any head rush—this is a seeing-stars-against-dancing-black-blobs head rush. I fall into an empty seat and put my face in my hands, praying that I don't pass out.

After a few seconds, the stars go away, but I still feel a little dizzy as I lift my head. And then I see him. The same man who was outside my hotel room this week—the short guy with the giant camera. He's right across the aisle from me, and he's snapping pictures!

"Stop it!" I scream, ready to cry. "Who are you?"

But he just keeps his shutter clicking as I lunge at his camera. He jumps up and sprints down the car as we pull into the next station. Then he turns and pops his flash one more time before he disappears through the doors.

I sink back down into my seat, teary-eyed and angry. That man actually watched me almost faint, and then—instead of rushing to my aid—he took pictures of me! When I get to my stop, I'm grateful that the Metro is just under the hotel. I slip on my oversized sunglasses and go directly to my room, where I slide into my bed and under the covers. I'm exhausted. And whatever just happened was downright scary.

Brring, brring.

I wake up to the double-ring of the European phone, which I'm starting to detest. I debate not answering it—I cannot deal with Angela right now—but when I pick it up, it's Veronica.

"Ready to eat?" she says.

"What?" I say sleepily, still out of it from my nap.

"It's day three!" she says. "I assume your fitting went well, and now the pain is almost over."

"The show's tomorrow," I say.

"Right," Veronica replies, ramping up for another lesson in how-to-lose-five-pounds-in-three-days. "So tonight you'll need some protein to keep you going tomorrow. We'll get you a plain steak— very clean—with no salt or oil."

An image of a slab of beef flashes through my mind. "Mmm . . ."

"I knew you'd be glad to hear that," says Veronica. "We'll be up in ten minutes."

Later, as I devour my plain but delicious steak, I tell Sam and Veronica about the creepy photographer.

"Ugh," says Sam. "Don't flatter him. He's not a photographer— he's a loser."

"Yeah," adds Veronica. "What a jerk! It's so weird that he's like stalking you. Do you think he was waiting outside your fitting?"

"I don't know," I say. "I hadn't thought of that, but I guess it makes sense."

"Creepy," says Sam.

"I had a paparazzo follow me around one year," says Veronica. "I was totally annoyed by him—he was, like, *everywhere* I went—but it turned out he was doing this really cool piece for a U.K. magazine about my street style. So maybe this guy's just doing something like that."

"By knocking on my hotel room door?" I say. "It seems extreme."

"Well, you never know," says Veronica. "Besides, you shouldn't be worrying about it. You've got the biggest show of your career to-morrow!"

"Yeah!" screams Sam, jumping up on the couch. "Tell us about the closing gown for Mirabella Prince!"

We dissolve into laughter as I describe the tear in Mirabella's eye when she saw her own creation being worn. "Such an egomaniac," says Veronica, who then goes into a story about how there was a but-ton missing from one of the blouses she was being fitted for today. "You would have thought the assistant had pissed on the thing, from the way she got yelled at," says Veronica. "These designers are more and more shameless each year." Sam had her own tales of woe—including how one of her designers is paying her in clothing instead of cash—and we open a bottle of champagne from the minibar as we talk into the night. When I finally fall into bed, I'm happy that Veronica and Sam are still in the living room, fast asleep on the divan and one of the couches. It's nice to have a sleepover in Paris.

We have to wake up at seven thirty A.M. the next morning—Veronica, Sam, and I all have shows today. We decide to be social and go down to the lobby for the continental breakfast—bread, jam, and coffee.

"Can I eat this?" I ask, holding up a croissant for Veronica's approval.

"I think you'd better," she says quietly, motioning behind her. I lean around her shoulder and see three men armed with cameras, snapping shots of me, Veronica, and Sam by the buffet.

Sam shrugs, "Eh, it's Fashion Week," she says.

But when we get to our table, we realize it's more than that. Sitting next to my plate is a British tabloid newspaper, and though I'm not the front photo, I can tell by the across-the-top headline that there is going to be trouble:

"FASHION ROLE MODEL STARVING! SEE VIOLET GREENFIELD, p. 7."

"Oh my God," I whisper, as I open up to a spread of photos. There's me at the door of my hotel room, looking—I'll admit—scary skinny in just my silk slip nightgown; there's me on the Metro, gripping a pole to hold myself up and then looking pale and sick in a seat as I try to recover from the near-faint; there's a shot of the fish and veggies I didn't finish the other night—he must have waited outside my room until we were done with room service! Ew!

The main photo, however, is the worst. It's me on the Metro, lunging angrily at the photographer, my face screwed up with fury and my mouth wide open as I scream at him. The caption for that one is, "HUNGER RAGE?"

The small paragraph of text explains how I was quoted earlier in the month about taking a stand on healthy body images for models, but now it looks like I'm starving myself for Paris Fashion Week. The saddest part is, the story is pretty accurate.

I look up at Veronica and Sam, who are both sitting silently and concentrating really hard on their croissants.

"Shit, you guys," I say, feeling the tears welling up in my throat. "What am I supposed to do now?"

"It's continued . . ." whispers Sam.

"What?" I say.

"The story," she says. "It's continued on page nine."

I turn the page and feel my stomach tighten. "RUNWAY MODEL DATING BRAZILIAN FASHION HEIR," reads the headline. Next to it is a photo of me and Paulo—taken on a boating trip—and a caption with a quote from Paulo about how we've been seeing each other since I walked his show in São Paulo. What?!

"Are you still *dating* him?" screams Veronica, way too loudly.

"No!" I whisper-yell back. "Would you please lower your voice?!" I'm now fully aware of the photographers milling about our table. And I'm determined not to let them see me sweat. "This picture is from months ago—I haven't even spoken to him since August!"

"It's just Fashion Week filler," says Sam, squeezing my hand supportively. "Seriously—don't worry. No one will care."

Well, I can kiss the Mirabella campaign good-bye, I think to myself. I haven't mentioned it to Veronica or Sam because I'm afraid one of them might be up for it too. It's weird to have friends who are also your competition. "Can we go upstairs?" I ask. "I've got to get out of here."

"Yes, babe," says Veronica. "But first—for the cameras—polish off that croissant."

I pop the buttery morsel in my mouth and stand up. Sam and Veronica follow as flashbulbs trail us to the elevators, where—mercifully—the concierge asks the photographers to leave.

The second the elevator doors close I start thinking out loud. "This is my worst nightmare," I start. "This is exactly what I was afraid of when I agreed to do this ridiculous crash-dieting thing. I mean, why would I do that to myself while simultaneously trying to promote a healthy body image? Who the hell thought that was a good idea?!"

Veronica and Sam raise their eyebrows guiltily.

"I don't blame you guys!" I say. "I'm not the same girl who came to New York last year, naïve and easily influenced. I can make my own decisions."

"Well, I'm still sorry, V," says Veronica. "Nothing like this has ever happened to any of the girls as far as I know."

"Great," I say. "So I'm just the one with bad luck?"

"No," says Veronica. "That's not it. Nothing like this has happened to any of us because none of us have ever taken a stand for something we believe in like you have."

I stare at her warily as the elevator doors ding and we walk out into the hallway together.

"It's true," says Sam. "You spoke out about an issue that was important to you—that was brave."

"Maybe it was just stupid," I say.

"Don't think that way," says Veronica. "You've got a show to do—don't let some stupid Eurotrash tabloid make what you stand for mean any less."

"I think I took away its meaning when I agreed to starve myself," I say, opening the door to my suite. I look back at Veronica and Sam, who are standing in the doorway. "I've got to get ready," I say, closing the door on their concerned faces. I need to be alone.

twenty-one

I throw on a cotton shift dress and flats, plus a huge pair of sunglasses and a floppy sun hat that I have from one of the Madrid gift bags. Celebrity incognito is an obvious look, but it's better than letting those photographers see my true expression, which is one of utter sadness and confusion. I suddenly feel like I understand Britney Spears and her kooky outfits a little better.

I hurry outside to the car that's waiting to take me to Mirabella's show, which is being held at Le Carrousel du Louvre, some sort of underground mall. When we arrive, I get a glimpse of the runway as I hustle backstage, and I see that it's a patent-leather blue—really reflective and shiny. I hope it's not as slick as it looks.

As hair and makeup people bustle around me—teasing and combing, smoothing and smearing—I slump down in my chair. I'm too emotionally drained to manage the polite ritual of asking their names today. *I have to go through with this show*, I keep telling myself. *From this point on, I will* not *crash-diet, I will treat my body in a healthy way, I will be a good role model.* Looking around at the other girls backstage, I wonder how many of them are feeling faint from days of food deprivation.

Suddenly, a model I recognize from New York shows comes up to me. "Violet?" she asks tentatively.

"Yes," I reply.

"I'm Ciji," she says. "We met last year in New York. And this is Heidi."

An equally stunning face appears next to Ciji's.

"We have a question for you," says Heidi.

"Okay," I say, wishing I didn't have to interact with anyone today. Wishing I could curl up and watch a VH1 marathon on the couch with Roger, who always knows how to just be there, without having to talk.

"Are you still with Paulo Forte?" asks Ciji.

My heart sinks.

"Because our friend Becky says that she's been with him for, like, three weeks now," says Heidi, crossing her arms.

"Yeah," affirms Ciji. "But then in the paper today—"

"Listen," I say, standing up from my chair and bumping the poor hair guy who's been teasing for half an hour now. "I have no idea why that was in the paper. If you want to ask someone about it, ask Paulo. I haven't spoken to him in months."

Ciji and Heidi back off a little bit.

"And another thing," I say. "It's true that I did diet some for this show, but that doesn't mean that I don't think we should all be promoting a better body image for girls who are into fashion. I am completely—"

"Oh, we don't care about that," interrupts Ciji.

"Yeah, so you ate a little less in the days before the show," says Heidi. "Who didn't?"

She and Ciji look at each other and laugh as they walk away.

Brring-brring. I pick up my cell phone, fairly certain of the voice I'll hear on the other end.

"Vain Violet," sings Angela, in better spirits than I expected. "Caught your exposé today. Quite impressive."

"Angela," I say. "I'm sorry. I didn't know—"

"Oh, shush darling," she interrupts. "I actually thought the angry photo of you was quite spectacular. Remind me to set up a moody shoot for you when we get back to the States."

"So you don't care that I seem hypocritical after telling all those reporters that I was going to take a stand about being healthy as a model?" I ask.

"Not in the least, darling!" says Angela. "Tryst has already issued a statement saying that you've been suffering from exhaustion and a touch of dehydration for the past few days—that will be sent out over the wires in case any U.S. news outlet wants to make more of this than there is. I realize that you didn't do an interview this time. We can't stop the persistent paparazzi! Besides, it's a big honor that they're interested in you at all, so I'm just going to let this one wash over me. Though I don't know what you're doing with that Paulo Forte . . . I suppose he's a bold enough name for now. When we get back to New York, though, I'd really like you to go for someone bigger—Leo perhaps? Or that Ryan Gosling? Whoever's hottest these days."

"But, Angela, I'm not back with—" I start to explain how I haven't seen Paulo since August, but, as usual, Angela has hung up already. I'm glad she's not mad, and I'm starting to think that maybe I'm making too big a deal out of the photos in the paper. Maybe no one else cares about the hypocrisy of my situation.

I sink back into my chair and hair guy continues to tease. I look at his reflection in the mirror.

"Hi," I say to him. "I'm Violet."

"Julian," he says, smiling. "Nice to meet you."

I nod and grin, ready to revert back to my dull mirror stare and ponder my fate as a near-anorexic role model for positive body image. But Julian has other ideas.

"So this is like a really, really big show," he says, showing a giddy factor that's unusual in jaded Fashion Week hairstylists. "I mean, really big."

"Yeah, I guess it is," I say, sitting up straighter and wondering why he doesn't have a French accent. "Hey—where are you from?"

"Ohio," he whispers into my ear, looking around like he's giving me secret spy information that he's afraid someone will overhear. "I was plucked from obscurity to come here!"

"Really?" I say. "Me too."

"Oh, not really," he continues. "I mean, I moved to New York to start a career in hair and I just ended up with a few great internships where I assisted big names. Then, one of Mirabella's people dropped out last minute, and here I am, teasing the tresses of Miss Violet Greenfield!"

He shrieks that last part, and I can't help but giggle at his enthusiasm.

"I'm just a girl from Carolina," I say. "Nothing special about my tresses."

"Oh puleeze!" Julian snorts, waving his comb around violently. "You're only the girl who's closing Mirabella Prince's show in the much-talked-about golden gown. Can you tell me what it looks like? I won't spill—I swear!"

"I guess I shouldn't," I say. "But you'll see it for yourself in about an hour."

"Oh, you're a good girl," Julian says, smiling. "Too bad!"

"I'm not that good," I say, frowning.

"Don't let those bitches get you down," says Julian. "I saw the paper too. That Paulo fool is just trying to link his name to yours now that you're walking the hottest runway in Paris. Girl, you're a superstar. You are going to *kill it* in that gold dress."

"Thanks," I say quietly.

And suddenly, with Julian finishing up my hair teasing and smoothing out my almost-splitting ends, I catch a little of his enthusiasm. So what if I ate a little less over the past few days? When I set my mind to it, I lost the damn weight, didn't I? Besides, I am walking a runway for Mirabella Prince in *Paris*. Pinch me.

The dress that I'm wearing is so heavy that there's no way I could walk twice—there'd be no time to get me out of another outfit and into this metal contraption. Yes, it's couture, and it's beautiful, but it's really freaking hard to wear.

If the fittings girl says "Beauty is pain" one more time as she pokes me with her pins, I'm going to scream. The New York dressers never once touched my skin. "Ouch!" I snap at her. "Watch your fingers!" Then I smile to myself. Something about this dress, this show, the prospect of this huge campaign, is turning me into a diva.

The hush of the crowd during Mirabella's show is so complete that I can almost hear the silence. I can feel my heart beating through the couture as the wardrobe girl makes her final adjustments and Julian does a last-minute tease touch-up.

There's a gust of wind as Angela bursts backstage, and I cringe, thinking she's going to chastise me after all. But she merely air-kisses both of my cheeks and says, "This is your moment, Golden Violet," before she ducks back out to her seat.

When I step onto the blue lacquered runway, which is totally going to make my dress shine, I can hardly hear the strains of an old French opera that Mirabella has chosen for the show. My own heartbeat in my ears is louder than the gasps, the ooohs, and the "oh my"s that I can read on the front-row lips. Although my feet don't show, Mirabella insisted that I wear four-inch golden heels that buckle up my leg to the knee—they're extremely stiff and hard to move in, but I can tell that my image has everyone captivated. I'm not even worrying about my walk. I have this strut down. I have these people in the palm of my hand. I own this runway. *I am a golden goddess.*

Then, just to my left at the end of the runway, I catch a familiar face in the front row. *Is it? It can't be . . . but it is.* Paulo. The memories of our runway kiss, days on the beach, nights in the pool house run through my head. Suddenly, my knees buckle . . .

The harsh stage lights swirl above my head and I hear frantic shouting as I feel the ground disappearing from beneath me. A strong hand grabs my arm, but it's no use. I can't believe it. *I'm fucking fainting.*

twenty-two

EMTs . . . Angela's bright red lips yelling "Wake up!" as her red fingernails slam together in a vicious clap . . . Mirabella taking a bow without me while blowing kisses as I ride out on a stretcher that they have backstage for twiggy models who don't eat . . . And Paulo's face.

These are the visions that run through my head when I wake up in my hotel suite with a nurse at my side, feeling my pulse.

"There she is," says the nurse gently. "You are all right, Violet, just a little hungry, *je pense. Oui?*"

"*Oui,*" I say meekly, grateful to wake up to her kind brown eyes and not the harsh, contact-enhanced blues of—

"Wilting Violet!" Oh. Angela *is* here. "Is it your mission in life to ruin yourself, and me in the process?"

"No, Angela." I sigh, not even trying to say more because I can hear by her tone that she's not going to pause for back-and-forth conversation. The nurse, probably embarrassed by Angela's vitriol, retreats to the bathroom to rinse her thermometer.

"Is it your goal to bring down Tryst Models—a premier agency for over fifty years—with your trivial, juvenile stunts?"

I shake my head no.

"Then why is it that I find myself here, in your hotel room, on the biggest night of Paris Fashion Week, tending to a silly, fainting little model instead of celebrating the most important runway show of the season?" Angela's loud whisper is just as effective as her full-volume growls.

"If there's a party you need to go to, you're free to—" I start.

"No, no," says Angela. "I'm here with you. And do you know why I'm here with you?"

"I'm guessing it's not because you want to make sure I'm okay," I say.

"Well," says Angela, pondering that thought as if it just entered her mind for the first time. "Yes, I did want to do that. But also, I am here because there are quite a few people right through those double doors who want to know how you are."

"Those doors?" I ask, pointing to the separation between the suite's bedroom and living room areas. "There are people in my room?!"

"Yes!" hisses Angela. "Lots of people. Very important people. So I suggest you get your skinny ass out of bed and put some clothes on!"

Is it wrong of me to smile inwardly when Angela says my ass is skinny?

I stand up quickly and realize that's a mistake as the nurse runs out from the bathroom to ease me back into bed. "No, no," she whispers to Angela. "She needs rest tonight."

"Well, in that case," says Angela, glaring at me as if she's a general whose battle cry I just left unheeded, "They'll come to you."

And before anyone can stop her, Angela throws open the double doors that have been shielding me from . . . well, the public.

As a blinding light and a camera crew rushes into my room, I make out the faces of Veronica, Sam, Julian the hair stylist—who are these VIPs Angela's so worried about? Then, lurking in the back, I see Mirabella and four men in suits and ties. I'm guessing those are the money guys.

But as soon as they hustle in, the nurse—who is slowly becoming my hero—starts yelling in French. I can't quite tell what she's saying, but whatever it is, it works. They hightail it out of my room and she slams the door on them. Only Veronica slips through, and she's by my bedside in an instant.

"Oh my gosh, V, are you okay?" she asks.

"I'm okay," I say. "I just got a little dizzy. You know me and four-inch heels."

Veronica smiles. "Not to mention surprise visitors . . ."

"Paulo?" I say. "Yeah, what the fu—?"

"Shh," says Veronica. "Let's talk about this later. For now, I have something to handle with Angela."

"Veronica, you don't have to—" I start.

"I know I don't have to," she says.

Then she turns to Angela.

"I don't know what it is you want from Violet tonight," Veronica says icily. "But whatever it is can wait until morning. She fainted, she's dehydrated, and she needs to rest."

Angela turns to me. "Nurse Ratched here is pretty tough, huh?"

"Angela, I *am* really tired," I say, lying back on the pillow and hoping she'll just go away.

"All right, Violet-the-Victim," says Angela. "But if you lose Mirabella's campaign because of tonight, you'll have a lot to answer for back in New York."

"Good night, Angela," says Veronica, stepping in front of my agent so she can't fix her signature glare on me.

"Well, aren't you two a pair of Charlie's Angels?" Angela huffs, throwing her ivory scarf over her shoulder and picking up her absurdly large Chloe bag. "I'll be back in the morning."

Then—thankfully—she's gone.

Veronica pops her head out into the suite's living room and I can hear her sweetly explaining that I have to sleep, but she'll be happy to pass on any get-well wishes. When the crowd has cleared, she and Sam slip back into the bedroom.

"You should have heard Paulo," says Sam, rushing over to kiss my cheek. "*Oh, I'm an old friend of Violet's—she'll want to see me . . .* blah, blah. Gag me."

"What was he doing here?" I ask, sitting up in my bed.

"We really should let you rest," says Veronica, and I see the nurse nodding her head in agreement.

"Back for breakfast?" asks Sam. "And a full rundown of the evening's events?"

"Yes, please!" I say, snuggling down under my covers. And I guess I really am tired because, within minutes, I'm asleep.

I wake up really early—like six A.M.—feeling restless. Although I know it's against my better judgment, I lean over to grab my laptop out of its case. I haven't been online all week, which is probably a personal record, and I just need a fix.

First, I log on to myspace.com/violetgreenfield. Eek—743 new messages, 256 new friend requests, and 1,482 new comments. Kind of overwhelming. I scan through the first dozen comments. All are about my fall last night, but they're pretty nice, like, "Hang in there, Violet!" and "UR still my favorite model!"

I know it's totally masochistic, but since my MySpace fans have heard about the fall, I want to see what's out there about it. I Google "Violet Greenfield fall"—whoa. I click on a few links and find that there are three photos that seem to be the most popular with bloggers—one of me leaning forward toward the camera where you can tell I'm about to bust ass, one of me landing knees first on that blue-lacquered runway (though the dress still looks great, I think), and one of me being wheeled out on a stretcher. Okay, they're all pretty terrible. Even Trent from Pink Is the New Blog made fun of me—but in a good-natured way.

I'm poring over the editorial coverage—which is speculating about my weight, whether I'd eaten, the Tryst press release about my dehydration and exhaustion—when there's a knock at the door.

"Room service!" I'm a little skeptical, but I peep through the hole and see a waiter with two rolling trays, so I let him in.

Bacon, eggs, *pan au chocolat!* I realize I'm starving. As I tuck a cloth napkin into my nightgown, there's another knock. When I open the door, Sam and Veronica shuffle in sleepily, wearing tank tops and underwear—the model's pajama set.

We plop down on the couch.

"Jesus!" screams Veronica, staring at my legs. My nightgown has ridden up, and I look down to see two huge, purple bruises on my knees.

"I know," I say. "They're pretty sore."

"God, I bet," says Sam. "That was one nasty spill."

"Yeah," I say. "It's all over the Internet today."

"And the paper, I'm afraid," says Veronica. "It's outside your door."

"You know," I say, "I don't even care. I'm not going to look."

"Good for you!" says Sam.

"Yeah, well, I spent an hour online this morning reading everything," I say sheepishly.

"So what's the consensus?" asks Sam.

"Oh, that I'm clumsy or that I'm anorexic—or both," I say. "Anyway, whatever. Now one of you guys will get the Mirabella campaign and I'll get to go home. It works out."

"Uh-oh, Sam," says Veronica coyly. "Violet's pretending she has no ambition again."

"You mean like last year when she dropped the Voile campaign but then burst back on the scene the minute she heard the words *São Paulo*?" replies Sam.

"Exactly," says Veronica, grabbing a piece of melon. "V, you know there's a press conference in the lobby at three P.M. today where Mirabella's going to announce the face of her spring campaign."

"There is?" I say, a little too quickly.

"See!" laughs Veronica. "You do still want it! Besides, Sam and I aren't even in the running for this campaign. The only names I've heard are you and that Ella girl from Romania—and she's with Ford. That's why Angela's all up in your grill—she wants a Tryst girl to land this."

"More important, you're into it," says Sam. "I can tell."

"So can I," says Veronica. "And I'm going to ask you one more time: Do you still want Mirabella? Truth."

"No, really," I say. "I know it's not going to happen after last night."

"That's not an answer," says Veronica. And she's right. I'm avoiding it. And I'm avoiding it because of course I really, really, *really* want the Mirabella campaign. But I'm not about to admit that—especially since my chances are like zero.

"So thanks for ordering the food, guys!" I gush, hoping to change the subject.

"Nice diversion, Violet," says Sam, biting into a croissant and letting the gooey chocolate inside drop out the other end. "But we didn't order this."

"Yeah," says Veronica. "We were going to suggest it, though, so I'm glad it's here."

"Well if you didn't—then who—?" I look down at the tray and see a small, folded piece of paper.

Violet, please accept this breakfast and hurry to get well. I want to speak with you if you'll see me. I have things to explain. Love, Paulo.

I read it aloud and Veronica rolls her eyes. "Explain this, Brazil Boy," she says, holding up her middle finger.

"Can we still eat it?" asks Sam hopefully, pausing in the middle of a bite of scrambled egg.

"Duh," I say, tossing the note into a nearby wastebasket. "No use wasting good food just because the guy who sent it is rotten."

twenty-three

Angela called this afternoon, but I wouldn't let her come up. I don't want to deal with her right now. I just told her I'd see her downstairs. She was ranting and raving about how we'd lost the Mirabella campaign, how I was a loose cannon, how she should never sign girls over sixteen—"they're too willful!" It was a nightmare talking to her, so I hung up.

As I get ready for the press conference, I wonder if I should wear my long dress—the one with the dark, swirling prints all over it. Julie always says it's "very seventies dinner-party chic." Roger just calls it "the skinny girl's muumuu." It would hide my knees, but as I'm looking through the clothes I have packed, I decide to go with a mini shift dress. If I'm going to lose this campaign, I might as well go out looking tough. I'll show those photographers that I'm not embarrassed about the fall—I can laugh at myself. I grab some ankle boots that Veronica made me buy last year and pull my hair into a ponytail. I glance at the clock—*shit!* 3:07—I'm late!

I race for the elevator, and I can feel my hands shaking. I grasp my gold clutch tightly to steady them, and I take a few deep breaths. When the doors open, I walk out into a sea of flashbulbs. A man on my left takes my arm and leads me to the press conference, where he ushers me up to the stage area.

"Oh, no," I say, "I'm just here to listen."

He shrugs. He probably only speaks French. But then I see Mirabella next to the microphone, and she's motioning for me to come toward her. I walk up three steps to where she's standing on stage, and that's when I look out and see a crowd of reporters and photographers—as well as Angela, Sam, Veronica, and a ton of other models and agents. Veronica has a huge grin across her face, and Sam gives me a thumbs-up. I look to Mirabella.

"And here she is!" she says into the mike as she puts her arm around my shoulder. "Just as she has fallen for Mirabella, you will all fall for Violet!"

There's a roar of applause and I hear a loud noise behind me. When I turn, I see a curtain falling to reveal an image from last night— a larger-than-life photo of me completely eating it on the runway in the gold dress. Above my head is Mirabella's logo and the words *Mirabella, the Fall Collection.*

I turn around and smile. *I got it! I got the campaign!* I pose for the cameras, showing off my knee bruises while I answer a couple of quick questions about whether I was hurt. "No, I'm pretty inde-structible," I say, flashing a big smile.

Then Mirabella shushes the crowd and says, "Violet Greenfield is not only a beautiful girl. She is also a girl with a mission—one that Mirabella believes in, as well. Violet believes that all girls should have a positive body image, and that we in the fashion industry have a responsibility to our young fans. Our fall campaign will embrace the mission of self-confidence, health, and 'keeping it real.'"

Even with a French accent (which may or may not be affected), the phrase "keeping it real" sounds completely and utterly lame. I fight the urge to roll my eyes, and cringe inwardly.

It's one thing to get a campaign that's strictly about fashion. It's quite another to attach this "mission" to it—especially when I know they'll ask me to keep starving myself before the photo shoot. *Can I do this?*

When the photographers and reporters clear out, Mirabella pulls me aside.

"Darling Violet," she coos. "That was quite a stunt you pulled last night."

"It wasn't a stunt," I say, eyeing her warily. "I wasn't feeling well." I'm fighting the urge to tell her the reason I was half sick was because I spent three days starving myself to fit into her gold dress.

"Well," she says. "Your name is on the lips of everyone in fashion today. I like the idea of a girl with flaws, someone who might stumble a bit, as the imperfect face for the perfect collection, so don't worry that pretty little head about it. In fact, that stunt may have tipped the Mirabella scales in your favor—I mean, look at the turnout for this press conference." She gestures to the media people packing up their cameras, then quickly adds, "But don't go fainting again, dear. It's bad for the whole 'healthy-body' thing."

"Yeah," I say, looking down at my hands. "Actually, I kind of wanted to talk to you about that . . ."

"There you are!" I hear Angela's voice echoing through the hall as she bounds toward us. "My favorite client and my favorite designer—what a match made in heaven!"

More like a commission made in heaven, I think. And then I pause. This is going to be *a lot* of money. Like, movie star money. Like, pay for all of college money. And although my parents aren't exactly in the poorhouse, a few hundred thousand dollars could really help—especially since Jake will be going to college in two years too.

"Yes, a lovely pairing," says Mirabella, waving her hand at Angela dismissively. "Now, Violet, what did you want to talk to me about?"

I smile up at her winningly. "I just wanted to thank you for the amazing opportunity, Ms. Prince," I say. "I am extremely honored."

She smiles back at me and takes my chin in her hand. "Well, irre-gardless of your clumsiness, you do take a gorgeous still photo," she says.

I wince, but not because she called me clumsy. *Irregardless?* Ugh—that is one of Roger's and my "You know you're talking to an idiot if . . ." buzzwords.

"Have you seen much of Violet's print work?" asks Angela.

"I saw the Brazilian campaign," says Mirabella, responding to Angela but grinning straight at me. "I only hope I can get as much passion from her as Paulo Forte did."

She did not go there! I force a smile and exit quickly, wondering if the whole world, or just the Western Hemisphere, knows about me and Paulo.

Upstairs, I find Veronica and Sam sitting outside my room.

"All hail, the conquering supermodel!" shouts Sam, jumping up to give me a hug.

"Nice job, Greenfield," says Veronica. And I feel like I can trust that she's really happy for me on this one. I smile back at her.

"Mirabella still wants me to do the whole 'healthy-body image' mission thing," I say, opening up my door and inviting my friends in. We flop down on the couches in the living room area.

"So?" says Veronica. "Are we going to have to go over this again, V? It's like the best of both worlds—you get to work on a campaign, earn like, what? Five hundred grand? And further a good cause at the same time."

"Yeah," says Sam. "It beats the paid-in-clothing route."

"I know," I say. "But I still think it's lame that I'm going to be promoting self-confidence and this whole 'love-your-body' thing while I obsess over gaining one pound so I can keep the campaign."

I sigh and look at their not-very-sympathetic faces. "I guess I can't have it both ways, right?"

"Now you're learning," says Veronica, clapping her hands together. "Hey, let's go celebrate!"

"You guys go ahead," I say. "I just want to hang out here for a while."

"Violet, you've been in this suite for like eighty percent of the time we've been in Paris," says Sam.

"So have you guys!" I laugh, tossing a tasseled throw pillow at her.

"True," says Veronica. "But it's time to change that."

"Okay," I say, relenting. "Let's go out tonight. How about we meet downstairs at ten P.M. in the lobby? I just want to rest a little until then."

"Fair enough," says Sam, getting up and pulling Veronica to stand too. I walk them to the door.

"V," says Veronica as she walks out, "don't forget to eat dinner." She winks.

"Thanks, Mom!" I say, closing the door behind them.

I go back to the living room and sit on the window seat, looking down into the courtyard below. I know that Sam and Veronica mean well—they're definitely my best friends in the modeling world. So why do I still feel confused? I want the campaign. I want the prestige, the glory—and the money. I just wish I could shake this weird selling-out feeling.

Part of me wants to call Mom and Dad, like a little girl who needs advice. When I talk to them lately, I leave out anything remotely controversial. The thing is, when it comes to the modeling world, they just don't really get it. Besides, I think that being honest with them will make them worry. I have to call someone I can be completely straight with.

I pick up the hotel phone and dial Julie's cell. Voice mail. It's been over a week since we've talked, but I guess that's my fault as much as hers—I haven't exactly been calling home very often. Besides, we're used to talking online and I'm sort of avoiding that lately. So, no Julie. I pick up the phone again and dial the person I want to talk to more than anyone else in the world: Roger.

I get his voice mail too, and I'm both relieved and disappointed. We haven't spoken at all since Barcelona, which was just a week ago, but it feels like forever. I still have some guilt over leaving him at the hostel—but he must understand why I had to go. Right?

And then I wonder: why didn't I just invite Roger to Paris? He could have stayed in my monstrously large room, and we could have eaten croissants and sipped espressos every morning before I had to go to my fittings and photo shoots for the campaign. Roger would walk around with his hipster guide to Paris tucked in his back pocket, his thick black hair getting floppy now because he didn't bring enough gel to last through our European travels, and each night he'd have stories about the neighborhoods he'd checked out, the art he'd seen, the people he'd watched on the street. We'd meet for dinner and he'd describe everything with the craziest details that only Roger notices, and I'd laugh and laugh at his imitations of our waiter's French accent.

Oh my God—I really miss Roger.

But he didn't get it—he didn't understand why I had to leave. Will I ever have friends who understand both at-home Violet and Violet on the runway?

I curl up in the window seat and fall asleep with the sun in my face.

twenty-four

      I wake up to the sound of the hotel phone ringing. The sun has set. I look at the clock—eight P.M. I realize I'm starving as I pick up the phone—it's probably Sam or Veronica wanting to have dinner before we go out.

"Violet," says the voice on the line.

"Roger!" I cry, my heart beating fast. I can't believe I'm so excited to hear from him. "How did you get this number?"

"Your mom told me the name of your hotel," he says. "Can you call me back on my dorm line? I don't know how much this is costing."

"Yes!" I say happily, ignoring the icy tone of his voice. "One sec."

I hang up and run back to the window where I left my cell. It's weird having to look up one of Roger's numbers, but I haven't memorized his dorm phone.

"Hi!" I say when he picks up. "How are you?!"

"As well as can be expected," he says stonily. "I saw you called earlier. What is it that you need?"

I'm kind of annoyed by his formal manner, but I really do want to talk to him so I barrel ahead. "Well, first, I know I apologized in Barcelona, but I'm still really sorry about bailing on you," I say.

"Apology noted," says Roger. "Anything else?"

"Noted but not accepted?" I ask.

"Violet, let's move on," says Roger. "Do you need something right now or did you just call to rehash old grievances?"

"No, I—" I stutter, not sure how to respond to this robotic version of my best friend. "Well, I was hoping for some advice."

"I'm listening," says Roger.

And at that small opening, I tell him everything—about the dieting, the weird subway paparazzi, the runway fainting, the campaign, the positive-body-image message Mirabella wants me to promote (while staying pin-thin by any means necessary) and even about how I think the money would help out my family. The only thing I leave out is seeing Paulo, since Roger seems to really hate him. Besides, that's unrelated to the question at hand.

"I read about the faint," he says. "It's strange when you have to hear updates on your best friend through the *New York Post*."

"Eek," I say. "Sorry I've been kind of out of touch this week! But, do you think I should do the campaign?"

"Sure," says Roger. "Why not?"

But his voice is distant, and I can tell he's holding back.

"No really!" I say. "I need to hear what you think."

"No you don't," he says. "You want to hear that you should do it. And you've already heard that from your fabulous friends Veronica and Samantha, so what do you need me for?"

"I need to know that you think it's the right thing to do," I say. "This is a really big step in my career, and knowing that you support it would mean a lot to me."

"Would it relieve your guilt?" asks Roger. "Would it make you feel like you were a role model for all the girls who are going to look at your ad campaign and pinch their own waists wondering if they can one day be your size?"

"What?" I ask. "What are you talking about?"

"Have you looked at your own MySpace page lately?" asks Roger.

"Well, I saw a few recent comments this morning when I—" I start.

"I mean really looked at it, Violet!" shouts Roger. And suddenly the distance is gone from his voice. It is full-on, in-my-face angry. "Have you seen the girl who wrote 'U R soooo gorgeous! how do you stay so tiny?!?! I wish i had your body!!'? Or the girl who asked you if you ever take laxatives after a big meal?"

"I didn't really get a chance to go through all the messages," I say. "Angela's been asking me to stay offline and—"

"Well there's your answer," interrupts Roger. "Bury your head in the sand and pretend like you're doing something good for the world by draping yourself in ten-thousand-dollar dresses and staring moodily into the camera. Maybe after you earn all that money you'll be able to justify it when girls starve themselves trying to look like you."

I take a breath, feeling like someone just stabbed me in the stomach. And then I get mad right back.

"What the hell is your problem?!" I scream. "Why are you trying to make me feel bad for the way I naturally look?! You're just like everyone in high school who used to say I had giraffe legs and toothpick arms! But you're worse—because you're supposed to be my best friend."

And then I think of something to say that will hurt Roger as much as he just hurt me.

"Besides," I sneer. "You're just bitter that you kissed me and I didn't kiss you back!"

"Oh, believe me," says Roger, not missing a beat. "If I could take that back I would do it in a heartbeat. Because you're not the girl I wanted to kiss—I've realized that you're someone else entirely."

"Fuck you!" I scream, slamming down the phone and curling

into a sobbing ball, soaking the shiny silk sheets on my four-poster bed.

When Veronica calls me from the lobby, I tell her I'll be down in five minutes. I've dried my tears, depuffed my eyes, and put on the hottest dress I own—a backless black sheath that sparkles down the sides and makes my boyish silhouette look like a perfect hourglass. I realize now that no one from home understands what I do. If Roger's goal was to put the nail in the coffin of our already-made-awkward friendship, he can consider himself successful.

That night we hit a total of four clubs, all of which lifted the velvet ropes for us. By the third location, I can smell the vodka on my own breath and the only thing I want to do is get out on the dance floor. The French songs all have great beats, but it's when the good old American breakup tunes start to play that I really get into it—I sing "Since U Been Gone" at the top of my lungs, and though I never liked Hilary Duff's "Come Clean" that much, I realize I know all the lyrics. When a dance mix of Beyoncé's "Irreplaceable" starts, I scream every word.

It's only when a slow love song comes on that I take a break to sit with Veronica and Sam in our VIP booth.

"Wow, you are so getting Paulo out of your system, huh?" laughs Sam.

"Seriously, V," says Veronica.

"Yeah," I say, downing another vodka cranberry. I don't tell them that it's not Paulo I'm getting out of my system—it's Roger. How could he have said those horrible things to me? I stare out at the colored lights and my eyes start to mist over, so I get up again to dance. If I sit too long I start to think, which doesn't do anyone any good.

twenty-five

Veronica and Sam flew back to New York a couple of days ago, and Angela was going to arrange for me to stay in Tryst's model apartment, but Mirabella stepped in with a studio in the Bastille quartier, which is kind of scruffy-chic and so much more my speed. I can't imagine sharing a bunk with Tryst girls right now—and *French* Tryst girls?! Even more intimidating and uncomfortable. I'm happy to have my own space where I can get my head straight. I'm not exactly feeling like myself lately.

When I arrive at the studio apartment, the key is under an outdoor flowerpot, just as Mirabella promised. I walk in and am instantly charmed by the geraniums in the window, the sunny corner kitchen, and the fold-down Murphy bed that's fully made and facing a wall of gorgeous heavy-glass-paned windows.

There's a basket of bread on the counter, and I open the refrigerator to find a little bit of butter and Camembert inside, as well as a bottle of champagne from Mirabella. I tear off a piece of bread and grab the cheese, sitting down at a tiny round corner table by the windows to have a ridiculously French snack.

I glance down at the cobblestone street below and think of the opening scene in *Beauty and the Beast* when Belle is racing around and saying "Bonjour! Bonjour!" to everyone in the town. Julie and I used to love that movie, and we'd make Roger play both the Beast and Gaston, the evil suitor, while we took turns being Belle. I sent Julie a MySpace message telling her where I am in case she wants to get in touch or something. She wrote back that my address sounded fancy, but she hasn't called me at all. I want to talk to her so badly right now, but I'm afraid she'll say the same things Roger said to me—what if they've even talked about it together?—and I just don't think I can listen to that again. It hurt enough the first time.

The shoot for Mirabella is tomorrow, and there's a package on the table with the press release about my participation in the campaign. I open it and read the first few lines:

"I am a real girl. I love my body because it is strong. I love my body because it is healthy. I love my body because it is beautiful."—Violet Greenfield

Um, okay. Thanks for making up dumb quotes for me. The rest of the release is about my dedication to putting forth a positive message for real girls, and how Mirabella, as a company, celebrates the beauty of all women. *What a bunch of bullshit*, I think, as I crumple the release and drop it in the wastebasket. And I'm the biggest bullshitter of all.

The next day I throw on a pair of jeans and a white T-shirt with a light zip-up hoodie over it. I spent the night tossing and turning, and I couldn't give a rat's ass about how I look right now. I walk out the door without brushing my hair or washing my face.

I get to the studio about ten minutes late, and I'm greeted by Julian, the hair guy from the runway show.

"Violet!" he screams, way too loudly for eight A.M. "I'm doing you again!"

I muster up a half smile and sit down to have makeup done first while he flits about, asking me all sorts of questions:

"Did it hurt when you fell?"

"Not much."

"Did you think you'd lost the campaign?"

"Yes."

"And then were you, like, soooo excited when you found out you got it?!"

"I guess."

"Are you nervous today?"

"No."

"You seem kind of tense. Here, let me rub your shoulders."

"Stop!" I scream. Julian steps back with a scared look on his face. "Sorry," I say softly. "I'm just a little tired."

When he does my hair later, I can tell he's still rattled by my yelling at him. "I really am sorry," I say. "I think I'm kind of homesick."

"It's okay," he says, smiling at me. "It might even work for the shoot."

"What do you mean?" I ask, realizing that I haven't been prepped on the shoot at all.

"I was told to give you 'sad hair,'" he says, making air quotes with his combs and blow dryer.

I stare at him for a moment, and then we both start to laugh. "What the hell is sad hair?!" I snort.

"I have no fucking idea!" Julian cackles. "I'm going to do a Veronica Lake, in-front-of-face type thing."

"Perfect!" I say, staring back into the mirror. "And believe me, I'm in the mood to give them my best pout."

The shoot is in a plain white studio. Just me, no props. A year ago I would have been terrified—I remember feeling flawed and freakish at my first *Teen Girl* magazine shoot last winter in New York. But now I just feel sullen and angry. I'm not even sure if I'm angry at Roger, at Mirabella, at Angela, or at myself. Maybe all of us.

"Violet," says Mirabella, walking over to the hair and makeup area with two assistants carrying clipboards. "I've decided that the word of the day is *somber*. With this whole positive-message thing, we do need to keep in mind that Mirabella is a high-fashion label."

"Okay," I say, not really getting the connection.

"So you with a smile would surely come off a little . . . *cheesy*." Mirabella wrinkles her nose as she says that last word, as if even the sound of the syllables disgusts her.

"Right," I say. "Somber it is."

When she turns to walk away, clipboarded assistants on her heels, Julian looks at me, deadpan. "Somber," he says in a pretentious accent. "Because that's the best way to make girls feel really good about their bodies."

"Yeah," I say. "Staring at them with a detached, maudlin face really says, *Love yourself, girls. Like I do.*"

Julian winks at me. It's good to have a friend on the shoot.

As I sit on the Lucite chair they've chosen as my perch, I'm not even trying. I'm just bored. And I look bored. And they love it.

"Gorgeous! Fabulous! Magnifique!" says the photographer, some semifamous guy who shoots for Italian versions of the biggest U.S. fashion magazines. I'm barely paying attention to the silly instructions he's giving me—"foot a little left," "elbow back on the right," "bend that knee inward"—and as I notice Julian trying to catch my eye every once in a while to make me laugh, I realize he's the only person in this whole studio who looks remotely real to me. It's like everyone else is made of cardboard. They aren't seeing me, they're seeing a paper doll under the lights who moves when they issue the right voice command. That press release talked about how I was the heart of this campaign, the spirit of the new Mirabella line. The truth is, heart and spirit have left the building.

When I finally exit the studio, it's getting dark. I plan to go home and tear off another piece of bread for dinner. I'm too exhausted to think about food. As I'm hailing a car, though, I hear a voice behind me.

"Violet?"

"Paulo?" I ask, not really able to make him out until he's standing right next to me, his face lit by the ornate streetlamp above us. "What are you doing here?"

"Listen," he says. "Can we have dinner?"

"I'm really tired," I say, glancing up and noticing that it's starting to mist a little bit. I can see the soft rain above even though I can't really feel it on my skin. That photo shoot must have left me numb.

"Please," he says. "I know I don't deserve to sit down with you, but I want to talk."

It's been a bad day. I feel like I signed the final check on my sell-out mission by posing for Mirabella. What could be better than to top off the evening by having dinner with the jerk who cheated on me last summer?

"Okay," I say, somewhat defeatedly. "Let's go."

I'm half expecting Paulo to lead me to a hot, new restaurant with purple lights and pulsing music where I can throw back a few shots and erase my memories of today. Instead, he takes me to a cozy neighborhood bistro with red-checkered tablecloths and small, nubby candles that look like they've lit a hundred deep corner-table conversations.

"First," he says, after we've ordered a half bottle of red wine, "I want you to know that I'm sorry. I never got a chance to—"

I stop him with a wave of my hand. I don't want his pity apology. "Paulo, it's fine," I say.

"You seem upset," he says. "It isn't . . . it isn't me who's upsetting you, is it? I will go if you like."

"It's not you," I say, sighing.

Paulo smiles. "You know, when I saw you faint, I thought perhaps it was my fault," he says softly. "Maybe I even hoped it was."

I laugh out loud, which may be a little offensive but it was involuntary. "It wasn't you," I say. "I hadn't eaten in, like, two days." And as soon as the words come out of my mouth, I realize that it's the truth. And in terms of Paulo, I'm fine. I mean, it's not fine that he was banging Skinnyskank on the night that I was planning on giving up my virginity to him, but in general, I'm okay. The hours of listening to the Paulo playlist on my iPod have abated, and now, sitting across from him in a tiny little corner of what is possibly the most romantic city on earth, I feel nothing more than exhausted.

He looks down at the table. *Oops. Maybe that dismissive laugh was a little harsh. Backtrack.* "I mean—even I thought it might have been you who caused the faint. I hadn't seen you in so long, and it was a surprise."

"I had very strong feelings for you," he says, lifting his head again.

"I did for you too," I say. "My feelings were so strong that I didn't even have to sleep with a slutty model to prove how strong they were."

Paulo winces. "A mistake," he says. "I didn't think you cared for me in the way I did for you."

"Really?" I ask, annoyed by his run-of-the-mill, lame excuse for cheating, but curious all the same. "Why would you think that?"

"Your eyes," he says. "They were always somewhere else."

"No, they weren't," I say, rolling those eyes now, as I smell a line of crap coming. "I was staying in your pool house, for God's sake, Paulo. Me and my eyes were always like *right there*."

"Sometimes," Paulo says. "But often when you were talking about home and telling me stories, I saw the light in your eyes come on. Even now, you're not here."

"Well, I'm homesick," I say, feeling my pulse quicken a little bit. It must be the wine—I really plowed through that half bottle.

"Exactly," says Paulo.

And maybe because we're in Paris at this absurdly charming bistro with red wine and bread and French onion soup, I suddenly get really sad. My eyes start to fill, but I swallow hard and fast a few times to get the tears to dissolve—a good trick I learned last year in New York.

After dinner, Paulo walks me back to my apartment, which is just a few blocks away. It's raining a little harder now, and even out in the brisk, late fall air I am still feeling emotional.

We say good night at the door to the flat, and Paulo kisses my cheek. "You are in my heart, Violet Greenfield," he says, before disappearing down the block.

The clock reads midnight, but that means it's only six P.M. on the East Coast. I want to call my parents, but I'm afraid they'll worry about me. Besides, there's only one person who's been able to give me good advice this year.

"Rita?" I say, my voice shaking as I hear my aunt pick up the phone.

"Oh, Violet, honey, are you okay?" she asks.

At the sound of her troubled voice, which is so often unconcerned and lighthearted, I start to cry. I give Rita a complete—if teary—rundown of Mirabella's campaign, why the whole healthy message part was important to me, and how I generally feel like a giant hypocrite who's letting herself get used. Then I tell her about Roger's phone call.

". . . And as much as I wished a night of dancing and drinking would erase the things that Roger said to me, it totally didn't," I say, finally clearing my throat a little.

"It just left you with a hangover, right?" says Rita sympathetically. She's the coolest aunt.

"Yes! A bad one," I say, almost smiling. But I'm not done with my story. "So today as I sat through that shoot, I could hear Roger in my head: *Why are you doing this? There are girls who look up to you—who want to be you. Why are you betraying them this way?* And I couldn't shake it. I could not shake Roger's voice."

"Did you think about the possibility that it was your own inner voice talking to you?" Rita asks.

"No," I say. "It was Roger. I could hear his condescending tone." Rita laughs.

"Seriously, Rita, I'm torn here. There are two worlds and I don't know which one is real. This one is full of money and spotlights and boys like Paulo Forte."

"And the other one?" she asks.

"You know," I say. "It's home."

"I know," says Rita. "And I don't think you've ever been torn. You know where your heart really is."

What a—to quote Mirabella—*cheesy* thing to say! "No. I don't know," I say, my voice cracking a little.

"Yes, you do," she says. "Your heart is with the one whose name makes your eyes look off to somewhere far away, as if you're next to him whenever you tell a story about him. The one whose voice is always in your head. The one who wrote you that letter I saw you fingering at my dining room table this fall. Roger."

I feel a tear slide down my cheek.

twenty-six

The next day I wake up to knocking. There's a man at the door, holding an envelope for me. It must be some proofs from yesterday's shoot. I'm kind of dreading them. I sign for two envelopes and bring them over to the kitchen table, where I watch the deliveryman drive off on his motor scooter. It's very Euro.

I tear open the first envelope and see dozens of pages of proofs—little black-squared photographs of me, thirty-six on a page—all with the same bored expression. The photographer has circled the ones he likes with an orange grease pencil. Usually, models don't see their own proofs—it's all up to Mirabella to choose the shots anyway. But Angela requested a set for me too, because she knew I was nervous about the shoot. She enclosed a note that says Mirabella isn't totally happy with the photos—she wants to rethink things a bit for the second shoot. Last year, news like that would have completely devastated me, but at this point, I don't really care. I toss the photos onto the bed and decide to take a walk around the neighborhood before I look at the other set.

I still can't let go of the weird, emotional feeling Paulo left me with last night. It's like the second I realized I was over him, another weight came down on me somehow. It makes no sense.

I walk to the river and climb down some stairs so I can get really near the water. There are artists along the bank painting with watercolors. One of them—an older man with ruddy red cheeks—asks me to stop. I understand that much, but I can't figure out what else he's saying.

"He wants to paint you," says a little girl who is passing by with her friends, giggling.

"I'm flattered," I say to him, "but I'm just on my way to—"

The painter has already unfolded a little stool and is motioning for me to sit. He reminds me of the poet Roger and I met along Las Ramblas in Barcelona, the one who wouldn't show us our poem until Roger paid him. What were the lines again? I don't remember it making much sense. I always feel awkward in situations like these, but it's not like I have anywhere to be, so I sit.

After ten minutes, the artist is done. He smiles and spins his canvas around. Although the girl in the painting looks more childlike than I think I do in real life—huge glistening eyes, soft pouting lips, and a sprinkling of freckles across her nose—she also looks quite a bit like me. So much so that I take in a breath as I examine it.

"How much?" I ask, pulling out a few crumpled bills from my bag. I'm not even sure what I have in my hand, but he takes a couple of small bills and I walk away with the painting. A bargain.

I carry it gingerly away from me as the watercolors dry, making sure it doesn't bump my leg. When I get back to the apartment, I set the painting up on the kitchen table, propped against a window. Somehow looking at it makes me feel better. The girl in it doesn't look like she's a bad person—she looks nice, like someone I'd know from home.

I flop down on the bed and flip through the photos from Mirabella's package. They're pretty good, I realize, in that fashion-ad kind of way. Being bored really helped me out yesterday, I think, but there's also an anger—and maybe some hurt—in my eyes that is pretty strong.

I reach for the second large envelope and my heart flutters—Julie's handwriting! It's not another set of proofs, it's a care package! Julie is completely famous for her care packages—she used to send me amazing things over the summers when we were apart. She was always at camp and I would be visiting relatives in the northeast. Even from camp, with like zero resources, she'd manage to put together a package with friendship bracelets, Sculpey-bead earrings, and a kick-ass collage every summer.

I tear into it quickly and find a handmade paper book called *Violet Greenfield, This Is Your Life (So Far . . .)*. On the front cover is a really great photo of me, Julie, and Roger on the Carolina campus—it's from the *Teen Fashionista* shoot, I realize. Julie must have pulled some strings with Roger's girlfriend, Chloe. My nose involuntarily wrinkles as I think of Chloe, but the photo is so cute that I almost forgive her for being lame. Inside, I find a few of the nicer clips from last year's *New York Post* stories about me, along with some of my runway shots that I'm sure Julie downloaded from style.com. There's also a photo of me and my dad with his coffee, and one of me, Richard, and Joanie at the theater—both from the *Teen Fashionista* shoot. Each one has a caption about different aspects of my personality—"silly," "sweet," "#1 daughter," "runway diva"—it's so great.

Then I turn to some newspaper stories Julie cut out from around the time when I was doing interviews about how my consciousness was changing, and how I wanted to be a positive voice for girls who look up to the modeling world. "Why make normal girls—who would never consider going on weird restrictive diets—feel like they have to be skin and bones?" I read over my quote and a feeling of pride mixed with shame washes over me. I meant that when I said it. That's what I really believe—not in crash-dieting or big-money campaigns. How did I forget who I really am so easily?

I take a deep breath in as I stare at the photo proofs spread out on the bed next to me. They're pictures of an angry, bored, listless girl. Then I look up at the portrait from the artist by the river, and I feel something rise up in me—it's a notion, just the beginning of something bigger, I think. But what it is is a sense of peace, a sense of knowing who I really am. And it isn't the listless girl in couture on the Lucite chair.

I pick up my phone to call Angela. I have to tell her that I'm dropping out of the Mirabella campaign. It's time to go home. For good.

I luck out and get Angela's voice mail, so I just leave a message for her. I basically say, "I quit. I'm going home." The funny thing is, I don't even care how she responds. She can rant and rave and scream her head off, but I'm out. Then I call Air France and try to locate my itinerary—it's like $600 to change my ticket date to tomorrow, but it's so worth it.

I suddenly feel happy, excited, like a weight is gone from my shoulders. I pack up my suitcase and lie back on the bed to look through more of Julie's scrapbook.

I find some photos from last year—our senior year—where I can still see my old self, the one who dreaded attention and shrank her shoulders inward to seem less freakishly tall. There's a shot of me in the Chapel Hill High School hallway pointing at the spot where someone scrawled "I ❤ VIOLET GREENFIELD" in tiny letters near the top of my locker. Those four little words had given me hope in high school—someone was thinking about me, someone noticed me. I remember wishing it was my old crush, Brian Radcliffe, who wrote it, but I never did find out.

I smile and bring the book closer to see if I can make out the inscription in the photo. Yup, there in black marker is that familiar lopsided heart that—

Lopsided heart. Where have I seen that before? I rush over to my suitcase and stick my hand into the side pocket where I stuffed the letter Roger sent to me in Brazil. It's still there, soft and worn because I've read it so many times. I open up the envelope flap, and there it is: "I ❤ VIOLET GREENFIELD." It's written in really small letters, just like on my locker. I remember not noticing it at first, but then seeing it upon a rereading of the letter and thinking Roger was being funny.

I take the envelope over to the bed and compare the writing on the letter with the graffiti in the photo of my old locker. It's the exact same. Roger was the one who wrote on my locker—way back in junior year. And he used to make fun of me about it! He'd laugh when I'd trace my fingers over it sometimes, absentmindedly. He knew how much it meant to me, but he never confessed.

What does this mean?

I pick up my phone and call Julie.

"Vi!" she screams, betraying in one syllable the fact that she's totally drunk in the afternoon. I can hear what sounds like a big party in the background. "I miss you so much! Did you get my package?"

"I got it, Jules," I say. "It's awesome, but listen, I need to ask you something."

"I tried to represent all the different parts of your great big life!" Julie continues, not recognizing the urgency in my voice. "Shut up!" she screams to someone who must be in the very loud room with her. "I'm on the phone with my best friend here!"

"Julie!" I shout. "I have to ask you something."

"What?" she barks. "I can't hear you . . ."

"Julie!" I try again. "Did Roger write the 'I heart' message on my locker?"

"Huh?" she yells.

"Did Roger write the 'I heart' message on my locker?!" I scream at the top of my lungs.

Silence. I wait for a few beats because I can hear her rustling around or walking somewhere or something.

"Julie?" I say.

"Hang on," she says. "I need to get outside."

I wait a few more seconds.

"Okay," she says. "Yes."

"Yes you're ready?" I glance back at the handwriting on the envelope—it *has* to be the same.

"No, yes is the answer to your question."

I feel a chill, like the kind you get at the part in the horror movie where the detective connects the final piece of the puzzle and realizes he's standing next to the serial killer. But this isn't a horror movie. It's my life.

"And you knew?" I ask. "Why did you keep that secret?"

"Oh, I don't know," she says in that low, slow voice people use when they are trying to make the person they're talking to feel dumb. "Maybe for the same reason that I kept it secret that he's been in love with you since first grade. Because he would have *killed* me if I said anything."

"He's been in love with me since first grade?" I whisper, almost to myself.

"Duh, Violet," Julie says, slurring a bit. "It was only so obvious, like, every day of our lives."

"But why didn't he ever say anything?" I ask.

"In case you hadn't noticed, our Roger has a major fear of rejection," says Julie, suddenly sounding more lucid.

I flash back to a thousand memories—catching Roger smiling at me in the rearview mirror of Julie's car, his visit to New York last year where he stood up to the jerk who was dicking me around, slow dancing at the prom, the long hug before I left for Brazil, his angry IMs, singing Backstreet Boys on the train to Barcelona—and that Kiss.

Oh my God—Roger loves me.

"I have to see him," I say, not sure what my plan is, but positive that I want to talk to Roger as soon as possible. In person.

"Yeah," agrees Julie, sighing. "Too bad he's in New York and you're in Paris. How internationally angsty of you two."

"I'll be in New York tomorrow night," I say. "Do you think he'll see me?"

"For you, m'dear," says Julie, losing her focus again as I hear her head back into the party, "he'll do anything."

twenty-seven

I have a really restless sleep. I am so anxious to get home—I need answers from Roger. But here's my biggest fear: I may have lost him. He was so cold the last time we spoke on the phone. What if it's all over? What if, when I finally find out that he loves me, it's too late?

I push those thoughts out of my mind as I shower. I've got a few hours before I need to get to the airport, so I take my time under the hot water. I've got my iPod on its speaker base, and I'm playing the song game, where I name a guy, and the next song that comes on is how he feels about me. Julie and I made it up when we were ten years old, and yes, I completely believe in its powers. I think of Roger, who's never been one of my song-game guys before. Right now, strains of the Pogues' "Tuesday Morning" are winding down— I wish I'd gotten that song for Roger. It's really good, and it's one of his favorites too.

"The next song that comes on is how Roger feels about me," I whisper. One of the rules in the song game is that you have to announce the guy's name out loud so that the universe can hear you and choose an appropriate song. Julie, who's extra hard-core, says that if a girl is singing the song that comes on, the guy isn't thinking of you at all—it has to be a male singer. That makes the game even riskier. She also would never condone playing by iPod—radio is much more random—but all I've got here is French radio and I don't have time to translate right now. I really need to know what Roger's thinking.

I cross my fingers and wait as the iPod starts up the next song. "Shot through the heart! And you're to blame..." Leave it to Bon Jovi to get right to the point. I sigh. This is a bad sign.

I turn off the water and grab my towel.

Knock, knock, knock!

Great, someone's pounding on the door and I'm naked. I wrap the towel around me tightly and peer through the peephole.

"It's me, you freak!" says a voice.

"Veronica!" I open the door and hug her, realizing that I'm completely starved for a friend at this moment. Then I start to cry. "What are you doing here?" I sniffle.

"I'm doing a shoot for French *Elle*," she says. "Angela, of course, wants to save money, so I'm shacking up with you. Or at least, I was going to, until I found out you're pulling the runaway act again."

"How did you—" I start.

"I spoke to Angela," she says. "Actually, I wanted to warn you: she's coming here. Like soon. She was so angry she could hardly talk this morning—I couldn't figure out what was going on, only that you'd quit. What happened? Is this why you're crying?"

I nod and blow my nose. "Sort of," I say.

"Listen, Violet," says Veronica, dropping her bag next to the bed and sitting down. "You're under contract here. You can't just up and leave. I mean, like, legally you can't."

"I hadn't thought of that," I say, sitting next to her and tightening my towel around me. "What should I do? I rebooked my flight for tonight."

"Is this about the whole body-image campaign and you feeling hypocritical?" asks Veronica, picking up the proofs that I left by the bedside and flipping through them casually.

"In a way," I say. And then I explain how it's about me realizing who I want to be—someone who speaks up, like I did in Madrid, and then sticks to her principles. "I got swept away by the glamour and the money," I say. "*Again*. I feel like I'm letting down everyone who cares about me, including girls who don't even know me but think I'm trying to do right by them. And I left my best friend—who flew like thousands of miles to see me—alone in a hostel in Spain just because Angela snapped her fingers. I can't believe I did that."

"Roger?" asks Veronica, looking up from the proofs.

"Roger," I say. "Julie just told me that he's apparently been in love with me like forever. I never knew and—"

"Duh," says Veronica. "And you've been in love with him . . ."

"I have not!" I interrupt.

"Oh, I'm sorry," she says. "I thought we were done hiding our feelings."

"I wasn't hiding anything," I say. "Roger's my best friend. I guess I just never thought of him that way."

"And now that you have?" Veronica asks.

"I don't know," I say. "But I need to see him."

"I can't believe this, Greenfield," Veronica says, smiling and shoving my bare shoulder.

"What?" I ask.

"You're going home for a guy!" she laughs.

"I am not!" I say. "I'm going home on my principles! I can't do a campaign that's pretending to help girls with their body image while the label's designer winkingly asks me to lose weight. It isn't right."

Veronica smirks at me. "Okay," she says. "I do believe that has caused you a lot of grief. But you have to admit that you didn't actually change your plane ticket until this whole Roger revelation happened."

"Can we call him the catalyst, but not the full reason?" I ask sheepishly.

"Deal," she says. "Now, there's one last thing to work out here. Get dressed."

I stand up and head back into the bathroom. "What's left to work out?" I ask.

"A little problem named Angela," says Veronica. "But don't worry—I have an idea."

Veronica and I are standing in the Hotel le Fleur bar, which has a chic minimalism thing going on. Lots of hard boards masquerading as couches and very little color. I notice that there are ivory marble eggs like my grandmother used to collect in a bowl on the bar. Veronica hasn't told me her plan yet, but we did leave a note on the apartment door for Angela, asking her to meet us here. "Neutral ground," said Veronica when I asked her why.

As we sit on a wooden-plank sofa that's more style than comfort with tiny cups of chamomile tea from the bar, I look up and see Mirabella striding toward us.

"What is she—?" I start.

"Let me do the talking," says Veronica.

I cringe, but agree to clam up. I've gotten myself in enough trouble for one week.

"Violet, Veronica!" says Mirabella warmly, clapping her hands together and leaning over to give us two air-kisses each. She obviously doesn't know about my plan to pose-and-ditch her campaign.

"Mirabella," says Veronica, flashing the stunning smile that made her famous at just sixteen years old. "I'm so glad you could meet us."

"Well, I was curious when you called," says Mirabella, looking at

Veronica questioningly. Then she glances at me. I make my face freeze in a smile—better to pretend I know what's going on.

"We have something to propose to you," says Veronica. "Don't we, Violet?"

"Uh . . . yes," I say, failing to sound resolute.

Then Veronica reaches into her bag and pulls out the scrapbook Julie made for me. *Is this her big plan? To show Mirabella my high school pictures?*

"I don't know if you followed the gossip pages last year," says Veronica, turning her attention to Mirabella, "but Violet and I were quite the pair." She turns to the *New York Post*'s coverage of our nightclub adventures—there were a few stories about me and Veronica included in the scrapbook. The press nicknamed us "Double V" and really got into the glamorous aspects of our nightlife. Of course, they also labeled me a prude and started a big feud between me and Veronica, but Julie didn't include those stories in the scrapbook—she has a nice way of wiping negative memories from the books.

"Oh, how charming!" says Mirabella, poring over the clips in the scrapbook. "You're quite an alluring duo—I can see why Page Six followed you. You two are just the picture of fabulous youth!"

"Yes," says Veronica. "It really did make quite a splash in New York City. I just wish we could have somehow become 'Double V' for the rest of the world. Now *that* would be an international sensation."

And suddenly it clicks—Veronica is a genius! I lock eyes with her and she winks.

"Girls," says Mirabella, looking up from my homemade scrapbook with feverish eyes. "I've just had the most incredible idea."

Suddenly, I see a fast-moving, wild-eyed Angela making a beeline for our alcove. She slows slightly when she realizes Mirabella is sitting with me and Veronica. "Ladies," she says, nodding her head and smoothing her flyaway hairs back into place. I can tell she ran here from the apartment—Angela is never this disheveled. She's clutching the note Veronica left on the door, and it's crumpled almost past the point of recognition.

"Angela," says Mirabella, eyes still glowing with excitement about her big idea. "I'm so glad you're here. I have an announcement to make."

Veronica and I are still playing dumb, smiling sweetly and sitting on the edge of our seats in mock anticipation. Angela glares at me and I give her a little shrug. Then she settles into a chair across from us.

"Now, Violet, I don't want you to get upset," says Mirabella, turning to me with concern. "But we did get such gorgeous shots of you the other day—you are a complete professional."

"Thank you," I say.

"And, Veronica," says Mirabella, "You've always been a Mirabella Prince girl—someone we've considered time and again when we cast the campaigns. It's just that the moment has never been quite right."

"I see," says Veronica, acting coy.

But Mirabella raises her hand to stop Veronica. "Until now . . ." she says.

Angela's eyes widen as Mirabella faces her.

"Angela, what would you think if we used the Double V for our campaign?" asks Mirabella. "Both girls—some shots of Violet and some of Veronica. Of course it would mean reworking the contract, but since both are Tryst beauties that shouldn't be a problem for you."

Before Angela can answer, Mirabella turns to me. "Violet, it would mean giving up some of the prestige of having this campaign to yourself—but I think Veronica will add a dash of energy to the project."

I look down at my hands, trying to pretend that I'm just considering the idea and I need to get used to it a bit. Which I guess I am. While part of me is doing cartwheels inside—this is the perfect plot for me to get out of my contract!—another part wonders about the message of the campaign. Will Veronica care enough to see it through? Will she be able to be a role model? It's true that she has come a long way since the coked-up-bulimia days of last year. I guess if I keep on top of her—if we sort of do this whole "love-your-body" thing as a pair—we'll be able to send a good message to girls. After all, we've overcome a lot together.

"I like the idea," I say, squeezing Veronica's hand.

"Yeah," says Veronica, looking straight at Mirabella. "You are a complete genius."

"You don't get to the top of the fashion world without a little ingenuity," says Mirabella, standing up. "I really must run, though, girls. Angela, I'll have my office send you a revised contract tomorrow."

Angela, who's setting a new record for silence, nods. She looks like she's in shock.

"Violet," says Mirabella, taking my chin in her hand. "You're lovely—a perfect beauty for my campaign. Veronica will only enhance your impact. And the two of you will spread the message of girl power even better than one."

Then she tucks her gold clutch under her arm and walks away, clapping her hands together and saying, "Best friends—the Double V—what a brilliant idea!"

When she's out of sight, Veronica smiles. "That woman takes self-congratulation to a whole new level," she says. "So, Ang, how about a little thank-you?"

I'm always amazed by the way Veronica can be so casual with our agent. I'm still a little scared that Angela's going to yell and scream, but then I see her face break into a smile and she starts to laugh.

"My girls, my girls," she says, throwing her hands in the air. "Bravo. Violet, I believe Veronica Trask just saved your butt. I was going to sue you if you left, you know."

I laugh nervously. Is she kidding? Sue me?

"I'm serious," she says, her straight white veneers in a perfect grin. "But now we can part as friends."

"Does that mean I'm free to go?" I ask.

"Free as the wind," says Angela. "For now."

I look over at Veronica. "See me off?" I ask.

"But of course," she says. "Excuse us, Angela. One half of the Double V has a plane to catch."

We leave our agent staring after us as we link arms and strut through the lobby together like the good friends—and supermodels—we are.

I make Veronica ride to the airport with me. When we get settled into our taxi, she says, "Tell me again how amazing I am."

"Your scheming abilities are beyond dazzling—you're a mastermind of first caliber, an unparalleled architect of brilliance." I reach out to hug Veronica for about the fifth time today.

"Aw, shucks," she says.

"And you scored yourself a pretty sweet contract in the meantime," I say, smiling.

"Everybody wins!" she screams, kicking her feet up into the air. She can hardly contain her excitement about the campaign. "Our Mirabella ads are going to break in *Women's Wear Daily*, then we'll be in spring issues of *Vogue*, *Pop*, Italian *Elle*, *W!* Violet, this is huge!" As I see her glee, I recognize that I never feel this kind of unbridled joy when it comes to the modeling world. I'm always super nervous or worried or stressed—or trying to convince myself that this is what I want. I feel a tear run down my cheek and I turn my face to the window so my mood won't spoil Veronica's moment, but like a good friend, she notices everything.

"V?" she says, touching my shoulder. "What is it?"

"Same old stuff," I say, wiping the tear away. "I'm just glad to be going home."

epilogue

When I arrive in New York, it's cold and rainy. I grab a cab and give the driver the address for Roger's NYU dorm. No IMs, no phone calls, I'm just going to show up at his door. I'm terrified, and I have no idea what I'm going to say.

When I get to the lobby I'm greeted by a security guard. "Um, Roger Stern's room?" I say.

"Ah, the party," he smiles. Actually, this guy looks less like a security guard and more like a student. He's probably my age. "It's on the seventh floor."

I smile and push the button for the elevator. As I ride up, I can hear shouting and laughing—and it's getting louder. When the door opens on seven, I walk out and immediately bump into a guy shotgunning a beer. "Fuck, man!" he shouts, giving me an angry look.

"Um, sorry," I say, stepping over his growing pile of Bud Light cans. There's toilet paper strung between doorways, girls wearing bras and beads (isn't Mardi Gras in the spring?) and a giant bong sitting in front of the bathroom door.

"Gotta piss, take a hit," says the guy standing next to the bong. "Entry fee," he whispers, smiling.

"Um, no thanks," I say. "Do you know where Roger Stern's room is?"

"Stern-o!" he shouts through the doorway across the hall from the bathroom.

Stern-o? "Oh, in there?" I say. "I'll find him."

I push through a few partygoers and peer into the room. There are probably twenty people crammed into a twelve-by-twelve-foot space, along with two desks and two beds, both of which are full of students holding yellow plastic cups.

"It's not about Sethe!" shouts a bearded guy with a bandanna around his neck and a T-shirt that reads SORRY, I DON'T OWN A TV. "It's about Baby Suggs."

I realize that this guy is having a hissy fit over something involving Toni Morrison's *Beloved*. I read it junior year. I laugh a little to myself and look around the room to find his sparring partner.

That's when I see Roger. His hair is a little longer—it's almost covering his glasses. He's leaning back on the bed and he has his arms crossed behind his head, the pose he takes when he knows he's totally winning an argument.

Then I see a hand on his leg. His thigh, really. And I hear it: the honking snort. It's Chloe. Chloe's hand is on Roger's leg. And I watch him lean forward and put his hand over hers, holding it as he smiles and stands up.

"Who wants another beer?" he asks.

I lurch to the right, outside the doorway and in the hallway where I'm out of his range of sight.

"Me, Stern-o!" "Dude, hit me up, Rog." I hear his friends—his new, college friends—asking for beers.

Roger and Chloe come out of the doorway and—thank God!—turn left. I see a keg at the end of the hallway. You know when you're in a moment where things are going on around you, and there's lots of noise and chaos, but you're kind of in a vacuum where you can hear your own heart beating and you're seeing people in slow motion? That's this moment for me—the moment when I see Roger and Chloe stop near the keg. They're both holding like four yellow cups, but Roger still manages to put his arms around her short little waist and lean down for a long, slow kiss.

I shut my eyes before they part, and I slide to the floor. No one has noticed Violet Greenfield, supermodel, at the NYU hallway party. Maybe that's because I'm wearing yoga pants, a hoodie, and no makeup. Or maybe it's because this was all a dream—I'm back to my old self: the wallflower whose best friend doesn't even see her anymore. A kind soul hands me a beer and pats my shoulder, though he doesn't stop to talk. I down the beer and then sit there, on the badly stained hallway carpet, for what must be thirty minutes. Roger and Chloe even walk past me a couple times, but I lean my head on my knees in case they glance down. They don't.

Finally, when I hear Chloe's snorting in the corner room by the keg as Roger tells some presumably beyond-hilarious story about his psych professor, I stand up to go. I walk slowly toward the elevator bank, and as I pass the third room on the right, I see a familiar poster: Ziggy Stardust. I smile in spite of myself and step into the room. It's less crowded in here—just a few people taking a break from the crunch in the hallway.

I spot Roger's plain navy bedspread, which Julie and I told him was totally preppy and boring. We tried to get him to take his Han Solo duvet, but even he realized that would be a dork move. On the corner of his desk I see a photo of the three of us—me, Julie, and Roger. Actually, my end of the photo is underneath the paperweight that's holding it down so you can't even see me, but maybe that's just by accident. *At least he hasn't cut me out of it*, I think.

"Violet?" I hear a voice behind me. Roger sounds completely confused, and when I turn around to face him, I think I can see both happiness and annoyance in his eyes.

"What are you—" he starts, and at the same time I say everything.

"I left Paris," I say talking over him but feeling unable to control the gush of words that's coming from my mouth. "I'm so sorry, Roger. I didn't know what I was doing. I didn't know what was important. I thought—"

And then a honking snort stops me. Chloe appears in the doorway behind Roger, carrying two cups full of beer and stumbling toward his bed. She flops down, somehow not spilling. Roger is silent, still staring at me as Chloe makes her entrance. I look over at Chloe, and her gaze follows his. She finally sees me. It takes a few seconds for her to register that I'm in the room.

"Violet!" she says happily, clapping the cups together and spilling beer. Maybe it *is* better he didn't bring poor Han Solo. I plaster on a smile.

"Hi, Chloe," I say, once again feeling supremely stupid for coming here. She's lying on his bed, for God's sake, like she owns the place. "I was just stopping by to say hi. But I'm flying home tomorrow, so I should get going."

"Oh, you're leaving?" she says, putting down one of the beers to grab my arm. "Stay and drink with us!"

"I really can't," I say. "I'm so jet-lagged, and my aunt Rita's actually waiting in a cab downstairs for me."

I turn to the mirror and pull my lip gloss out of my pocket—I don't want to meet Roger's surely dubious state. Why would Rita be in a cab outside? It's obvious that I'm inventing a reason to bolt. As I swipe on a touch of Paris Bubbly, I see something that makes me catch my breath. The yellow paper with peach flowers, the poem from Las Ramblas in Barcelona. It's tucked into the corner of the mirror above Roger's desk.

No mas que amigos; no menos que amor verdadero. I translate the words in my head as I read—"No more than friends; no less than true love."

My eyes dart to Roger's reflection behind me; he saw what I was looking at.

"Oh, hey," he says, walking over. "I've been keeping this for you." He reaches up and gently tugs the poem from the mirror frame, handing it to me.

"Thanks," I say. "Are you sure you don't want it?"

"Nah," he says. "I don't need a piece of paper to remember Barcelona."

I take the poem from him, trying to will my heart to stop beating so loudly, trying to act casual as I wrap my hand tightly around the soft paper and shove it into my right hoodie pocket.

I give Roger a quick smile. "Bye," I say. He looks at me for a moment, like maybe he wants to say something.

"See you at home for winter break?" he asks, giving me a grin.

"Definitely," I say, leaning in to give him a quick kiss on the cheek. Then I squeeze past him, step out into the hallway, and exit the party.

I grab my bags downstairs and I feel grateful for the cool wind that hits my face when I get onto the street. I'm planning on going to Brooklyn and staying with Rita before my flight back to North Carolina tomorrow. I'm not sure what just happened up in Roger's dorm room, but I do know that he's starting to forgive me.

When I get to Rita's house in Brooklyn, I ring the bell. Her porch light comes on instantly, and I hear her footsteps coming down the stairs. I take the Barcelona poem out of my pocket, just to look at it once more. This little yellow scrap of paper suddenly means a lot to me.

And now a special excerpt of the
next book in the Violet series . . .

violet in private

Coming from Berkley JAM
August 2008!!!

return to the red carpet

When we get to Marquee, Roger immediately gets in the press line. Two girls dressed in all black with clipboards and those weird head mikes are working the door. Their hair is slicked back into identical ponytails like those women in that old eighties video, "Addicted to Love." They're checking off names.

"Chloe put us on the list," says Roger, bouncing up and down on his toes like he's so proud of Chloe for being so ultra-special. I roll my eyes behind his back. I look around and see a lot of women holding designer bags that have a waiting list and wearing David Yurman jewelry. The fact that I recognize these things scares me. I'm not sure I want to be here.

But then I recognize something else—and I see a way to outdo Chloe. "Charles?" I shout to the bouncer at the door. He smiles slowly. "Violet! Come on through," he says, waving and lifting the velvet rope for me and Roger. I guess last year's exploits were good for something. Eat that, press line!

"Smooth," whispers Roger as we enter the club. I smile, but my moment of triumph is short-lived. Chloe bounds over and practically knocks Roger down with her voracious hug. *Could she be more annoying?*

I avert my eyes as they canoodle and I see a fury of flashbulbs in the corner. There's a giant *Teen Fashionista* logo backdrop and a short red carpet where the press is gathered to take pictures of the big names who attend the party.

"That's the 25 Under 25," says Chloe. "Veronica Trask is on the red carpet right now—they love her."

I push through the crowd to reach my old roommate, and I have to gasp when I see her. She's in head to toe liquid silver—a dress that drapes down to the floor with a deep V-neck that must require some major double-stick boob tape. Her sky-high cheekbones are catching the light and her dark-brown hair swings as her bright pink lips go from full smile to sexy smirk to pouty frown. The girl knows how to work a photo shoot.

I suddenly feel underdressed.

"V!" I hear Veronica's happy shout before I feel the heat of twenty flashbulbs turning on me. She grabs my arm and helps me duck under the press ropes so I can join her on the red carpet. Yup, definitely underdressed. We squeeze each others' hands as we pose together—the things I've learned over the last year come back to me naturally. I instantly go into the thin angle: pivot one hip back, elbow out to the side, head tilted slightly.

After a couple minutes, I tug on Veronica's hand.

"Enough?" she whispers through her smile.

"Yes," I whisper back.

We leave the red carpet to a few protest shouts, but then Hayden Panettiere arrives so they quickly forget we exist.

"How are you?" Veronica asks as we find a dark corner to talk in. "I see you decided to come down from college and visit your true love." She gestures at Roger, who's still standing with Chloe. They're both laughing.

"He's her true love now," I say defeatedly.

"Please," says Veronica. "A too-old flavor of the moment could never top your history. Besides, you're hotter."

"Thanks," I say. "I feel a little casual for tonight though—I didn't think I'd be making a press appearance."

"You look fantastic, as always," says Veronica. "Besides, in those heels you could wear a potato sack and make it fashion."

I smile.

"I'm glad to see you, Veronica," I say. "I just am not really into the whole 'being photographed' thing right now."

"V, with the campaign out, we've got to do as much press as we can," says Veronica. She sounds annoyed with me.

"Are you mad at me?" I ask.

She sighs. "I'm not mad," she says. I feel a "but" coming. "It's just that we're in this Mirabella ad together and I'm pulling all the weight. It's like you're already retired or something. People are always asking me where you are, if you're working . . ."

"Well tell them I'm in school," I say. "Don't people ever go to college in this industry?"

"Not while they're still on the rise," says Veronica. "Its like you're dropping out just when things could get really great for you."

But I already know this line—I've heard it from Angela. "No," I say. "It's not for me right now."

"Double V!" I hear a cheery Australian accent as I spin around to greet Sam, our third roommate from the Tryst model apartment last year.

"Group hug!" I shout, hoping Veronica will drop the issue now that Sam's here. Sam always lightens things up.

"You came into the city for the party?" asks Sam, smiling at me.

"She came into the city for a boy," says Veronica before I can answer. She's staring at Roger. He notices, and he and Chloe start toward us.

"What do you mean?" asks Sam. "Isn't that your friend Roger from high school?"

"I'll explain later!" I whisper hurriedly as RoChloe approaches.

"Hi, Roger," says Veronica, smiling in a way that makes me nervous. *Please don't let her say anything weird.*

"Veronica," he says, kissing her cheek. What a New York–party thing to do. How did Roger learn that?

"Hi, ladies!" gushes Chloe, leaning in to kiss both Veronica and Sam on the cheeks.

Before we can launch into awkward conversation, I hear a commanding voice from across the room.

"Chloe!" shouts an elegant gray-haired woman to our left. She's holding up her arm as if to summon Chloe. She's wearing a short, black dress with large rosettes at the hem, and a ginormous diamond cocktail ring flashes on her pinky. She radiates chic.

"Who's that?" I whisper, to no one in particular.

"Marilyn Flynn," says Sam out of the corner of her mouth. "The editor in chief of *Teen Fashionista*."

"And Chloe's boss," adds Roger. Chloe has rushed to Marilyn Flynn's side and is nodding rapidly. I strain to hear them.

"There's trouble by the DJ booth," says Marilyn Flynn. "I told you to watch Valentina around the champagne. Beauty editors always try to take over the music. Grab her!"

Marilyn Flynn waves her arm dismissively and Chloe is off like a shot, trying to head off the scuffle that's breaking out between the DJ and the beauty editor.

Then Marilyn Flynn sets her sights on our group. She steps into the circle. "Roy." She nods at Roger in greeting and he just smiles, not correcting her. Then he subtly slips away, like he knows this isn't his world. I watch him walk over toward the bar, and I wish I could join him.

"Veronica, you look stunning," says Marilyn Flynn.

"Thank you, Marilyn," coos Veronica softly. Sometimes she can be so oddly genteel. "You know Sam, of course."

"Yes, darling," says Marilyn Flynn. "Swimsuits last summer."

...am smiles. She always does swimsuit shots, which is why she spends half her time in Florida. I know she wishes she could move into other markets.

"And this is Violet Greenfield," says Veronica, gesturing at me.

"Hello," I say, not sure whether to hold out my hand or lean in for a party kiss or what. You'd think I'd know these things by now, but Marilyn Flynn doesn't move. I think she's a non-toucher.

"Of course I know Violet," she says. "Chloe profiled her last summer in a lovely piece. I've been dying to meet you, dear."

"Oh, thanks," I say. Then a long silence falls.

The way Marilyn Flynn is looking at me makes me kind of nervous, like I don't know where to put my hands or how to stand, so I grab a crab cake from a passing waiter. But then it's like, *I'm holding a crabcake with white sauce on top*, so I pop it into my mouth and focus on chewing daintily, which—if you've ever tried—is impossible. Chewing is not dainty. Just as my mouth is full of crab, Marilyn opens hers.

"So, Violet, I hear you're at Vassar," she says.

I work my jaw voraciously, trying to clear my mouth as I nod at her and attempt a smile.

"I always loved that campus," she continues. "Such lovely trees and gorgeous architecture."

Almost done with crab. Keep smiling. Chew, chew, chew. Swallow!

"Is your schedule very hectic?" Marilyn Flynn asks.

"It's challenging but not overly stressful," I say, praying there are no food remnants in my teeth while I give her the answer my parents seem to like.

"Her Fridays are free," says Veronica, smiling at Marilyn Flynn. "So she can do bookings then."

I look over at Veronica questioningly, and she winks. *Why is she trying to start something?*

"I was thinking less of bookings and more of an internship," says Marilyn Flynn.

"At *Teen Fashionista*?" I ask, stupidly. *No, at* Vanity Fair. *Duh!*

"Of course." Marilyn smiles, showing her pearly whites. "An editorial internship. I read your piece in the *Times*."

I look over to where Roger is still standing and trying to get a drink. I so want him to hear this conversation—I'm being intellectually appreciated here! Someone wants me for something other than my height and weight!

"Say yes, Violet," purrs Marilyn Flynn. "I've always wanted to have a model intern."

My heart sinks. But just a little bit. Even if she does want me because I've walked a runway, she also noticed my writing. I can prove that I'd be a great asset to *Teen Fashionista*.

"I'd love to," I say.

"Fabulous," says Marilyn Flynn. Then she claps her hands in the air. "Chloe!" she shouts.

Chloe comes running over from the now-pacified situation at the DJ booth. "Yes, Marilyn?" she asks obediently. Roger made it seem like Chloe ran the magazine, but I'm somewhat evilly satisfied to see her in this subservient role.

"Violet's going to start interning at *Teen Fashionista*," Marilyn Flynn says. "You'll be in charge of her."

I will my eyes not to roll.

"Great!" says Chloe, smiling doofily at me.

I can't read this girl. She could be like, "Great!" in her bubbly way and be truly excited. Or she may mean, "Great! Because I'm going to enjoy being a complete bitch to her in addition to stealing her best-friend-slash-true-love!"

I smile at Chloe as Marilyn Flynn excuses herself to chat with what is surely a more important group of people.

"This will be fun!" Chloe chirps when Marilyn's gone. So at least I know she's not faking it for her boss's sake.

I squeak out a meek, "Yeah," and grab Veronica and Sam, pulling them to the bar. "Excuse us," I say to Chloe.

...n I'm out of earshot, I start whining. "What did I just do?" I
..k them.

"Babe, you just took an internship at a great magazine," says
Sam. "An *editorial* internship—you'll probably get to write something for them!"

"But working under *Chloe*?" I look over at Veronica, who understands this Roger-Chloe-Me triangle infinitely better than Sam
does. Truth be told, Sam is kind of out of the loop.

"Violet, have I ever told you what my mother said to me when I
left for New York to start my modeling career?" she asks, eyes shining.

"No," I say, curiously. I've never heard a peep about Veronica's
mom.

"Keep your friends close, and your enemies closer," she says.

I look over at Chloe, who's huddled in the corner with Roger.

"Your mom is a smart lady," I say.

Berkley Jam
delivers the drama

Rich Girl: A BFF Novel
by Carol Culver

A new semester is beginning at Manderley Prep,
where being wealthy doesn't make you popular—
but it certainly opens doors...

Not Anything
by Carmen Rodrigues

After her mother's death, Susie Shannon closed herself
off from the world—until Danny Diaz helps her open
her heart again.

Twisted Sisters (Available April 2008)
by Stephanie Hale

Aspen Brooks thought that college would be a
dream—but between investigating a student's disap-
pearance and fending off her boyfriend's roommate,
who insists he's in love with her, it's turning out to
be one big nightmare.

Go to penguin.com to order!